MW01601652

BLEEK BLACKMON'S WOMAN?

A Black Cowboy Story

Angelia Vernon Menchan

Honorable MENCHAN Media L.L.C. 2023

Cover image by Maurice K. Menchan II
@menchan.Kreative@gmail.com

Writing Bleek's book was a labor of love for me. Something I never considered writing until I did. I'm grateful to those of you who choose to read it and review it because there are times in an author's life when something just a bit different is necessary to their spirit and creative process. Bleek was the medicine I needed. Enjoy.

#JustLove

Angel—

Bleek Blackmon III, stood at the window of the home he grew up in, staring out over the expansive property, property he owned.

His grandfather built the structure with his own hands more than eighty years earlier when he was a forty year old husband and father with an infant son. In those days it was a rare thing to see a Black man with his own ranch, a ranch with acres of land, horses, cattle and a field of vegetables as far as the eye could see. The first Bleek had worked twenty years and saved every penny to purchase the land and the livestock, forgoing love and a social life to have his dream. For a man born in 1900 it was a dream come true. Four years earlier he met and married thirty year old school teacher Alicia when he was thirty-six and she was thirty. His intention was to fill her up with sons but they were blessed with one son, Bleek Jr. who followed his father's path, down to marrying later than most at forty and getting his first and only son at age forty-one. Everything for them was about the land and legacy. Now it was all owned by Bleek III, who at forty had never married and honestly wasn't looking for a wife though his mother, Marie at age seventy-seven wanted a grandchild. Bleek recalled their conversation months ago after Bleek Jr. died at eighty.

Bleek, you won't live forever son. You need a wife and children. Otherwise what did your grandfather and father work for? All of this will get sucked up by sharks—the same sharks who would have, if they could have, stopped them from owning this land. Not only that, a woman, a good woman who loves you and can handle what you bring will bring joy to your life. You have everything else, son.

Bleek hadn't responded but he heard her.

What would that be like? Bleek wondered. *To have a woman of my own, a wife. Someone who could put up with what being married to a Black Rancher, a cowboy's wife in the twenty-first century.*

CHAPTER ONE

Anastasia Wright got dressed for her first day as the lead counsel for Blackmon Ranch. She was hired by Blackmon's retiring attorney, Roger Moses to replace him. She was surprised to be chosen, considering she just turned thirty-seven and the rancher business was known for being men only and very conservative. On the other hand she was an renowned lands attorney and served minority and women owned landowners and business owners well for more than ten years. Her brand was *Win The Wright Way* and win she did. The concerning factor was she hadn't met Bleek Blackmon III, the reclusive owner. He was well-known but an anomaly to most. He was stoic appearing and all business and as handsome as sin in his suits and cowboy hat.

He's probably a sexist Neanderthal. Anastasia thought. Staring at herself in the mirror. She was wearing slacks and with a shirt and light jacket, her hair up in a bun. She had twelve inches of natural hair but kept it restrained in business settings. Roger, her mentor told her to wear slacks, otherwise it would have been a dress.

¥¥¥¥¥

Bleek sat at the head of the massive table in the conference room. Roger Moses, his long time lead attorney was retiring and bringing his replacement to meet Bleek, his core office staff and Marie. His eyes narrowed when Roger walked in with a woman who appeared to be about thirty. His eyes raked over her beautiful face, to the uniform that looked conservative but could not hide the tall, shapely form. He met her eyes and saw the steely smirk on her face. He didn't break his stare—nor did she.

"Hello everyone. This is Anastasia Wright, my protege and replacement." Roger said. "She's the best and the brightest."

The four men at the table exchanged glances. There was Robert, the head accountant, Leon, the foreman, Nathaniel, cattle manager and Frederick, lead horse trainer. There was a huge staff but these were the decision makers. Marie smiled to herself, thinking, *She's a change maker.*

Ms. Wright, or is it Mrs. Wright, how old are you?" Bleek asked, his deep voice filling the cavernous room. Roger sighed and Marie chuckled under her breath.

"Mr. Bleek or is it Massa Bleek? I'm old enough to lead all legal concerns for your ranch and two or three others. Otherwise your retiring and esteemed counsel wouldn't have chosen me." There were a couple of audible gasps from a couple of people but smiles from Roger and Marie. "How old are you?" Bleek's expression remained stony but his eyes flashed.

"I'm forty. This is a ranch Ms. Wright and we don't take time for the proper words and questions necessarily."

"Perhaps, it's time you learned to Mr. Blackmon. By the way I'm thirty-seven and in practice for twelve years, the last six under my own umbrella and the prior under the tutelage of Roger Moses. I'm Ms. Wright." Anastasia said, she was still standing but pulled out a chair between Bleek and Marie and sat down. There was another glance exchange between the people in the room. The two chairs flanking Bleek always remained empty. Sensing something, Anastasia glanced around before asking, "Are the seats assigned or something. Mr. Bleek can a young woman attorney sit here?"

Marie threw back her head, allowing the laughter that had grown in her belly since Anastasia walked in fly free. Bleek scowled at his mother who blatantly ignored his glance.

"Ms. Anastasia, you will be just fine." Marie said. "This outfit needs a fresh face and yours is perfect. "I'm Marie Blackmon, do you ride?"

"Yes ma'am."

"If it's acceptable, I would like to get started on the business. I'm known as Bleek to my management team, Ms. Wright."

"I'm Anastasia." Formal introductions were made. Anastasia would be working closely with Bleek and Robert, the lead accountant. His executive assistant, Mena Rivers, a stern-faced woman in her late forties, came in to introduce herself and provide Anastasia with an introduction to Blackmon Ranch information.

"Anastasia, I'm quiet and don't mix or mingle much." Mena said. "I'm also dedicated to your success as you need me."

"Thanks Mena, I appreciate that." Anastasia said before focusing on those at the table.

Anastasia gave her presentation, impressing everyone with how much she knew about ranching, horses and land management, including the massive Equestrian Center that was new to the area. They had acquired thousands of acres of land for pennies on the dollar but chose to work closely with Blackmon rather than try to acquire his land. Blackmon land had certain codicils such as originally being Native American land owned by the first Bleek's ancestors which passed on and was protected. She was even more knowledgeable about Blackmon Ranch Enterprises. Bleek was more impressed than he wanted to be.

"Anastasia, your knowledge astounds me. Either you're going to be a major asset or you're an infiltrator." Bleek said. Anastasia stared at him several minutes before returning to her presentation, her eyes flashing.

"Everything I discussed is available in legal and certified documentation which will be provided to everyone. I need to get to work." She pushed back her chair and stood, facing Bleek. "Mr. Bleek, I could have worked for the other side, no infiltration needed. They offered me a salary of more than three million dollars annually but I made it clear to them and I'll make it clear to you, I work for minority businesses exclusively and I'm no money whore, selling my soul to anyone and it's not available to Blackmon Ranch either, just my expertise and knowledge. Have a good day." She slowly gathered her things, taking time to place them in her leather satchel before leaving to room to go to her office.

What an asshole? She thought.

"And that is that." Marie said before leaving the meeting. Bleek's expression hadn't changed but Anastasia's words pricked him. His gut told him she was on the up and up but something about her agitated him. He wasn't used to being agitated.

"Roger, she better be everything you say she is. She has a two year nonbreakable contract thanks to *you*." Bleek said, his tone harsh.

"She's more and you won't run her off with your—whatever the hell." Roger said. He was the same age as Marie and considered Bleek like his own family. Bleek ignored him, turning his focus to Frederick.

"Frederick, get her a great horse, a chestnut Irish thoroughbred."
Every eyebrow in the room lifted. Only Bleek and Marie rode and owned those horses. They were considered the best. "Meeting dismissed."

Bleek glanced at the clock noticing it was nine thirty am, the meeting lasted one hour. It was time to get BB and ride the ranch, his favorite Black beauty. Everyone thought he arrogantly named BB for him because he owned Bleek's Brand but the initials were for Bleek's Baby, which would likely have brought more ridicule. His guys respected him but gave him trash talking when it was needed.

¥¥¥¥¥

After a three hour ride, Bleek showered and changed into jeans and a pale blue dress shirt. He made a point of eating with his workers regularly in a massive kitchen and dining area that looked like a log cabin. He phoned Mena, telling her to bring Anastasia to what they called the canteen.

Anastasia looked around the massive dining area, the scent of grilled meat permeating the air, making her mouth water. The tables were long polished wood and about fifteen men, mostly Black but a couple of Mexican and one white man were scattered at two of the tables. Bleek sat at the end of one where Mena led Anastasia. Bleek stood, "Men, this is Anastasia Wright, she's replacing Roger Moses as my lead lawyer." Every hat in the room was tipped in her honor. She grinned and saluted them. "Ms. Anastasia, these are the men who run things, the cattleman, horsemen and life's blood of this ranch."

"It's nice to meet you." Anastasia said. She walked around and shook every hand before returning to the table. An older Asian man appeared at the table.

"Ma'am, what would you like?" He asked, his voice heavily accented, his expression inscrutable.

"I saw someone with a steak sandwich on whole wheat, I want that with tomatoes and onions, no condiments and vegetables."

"Cabbage, greens or peas?"

"Cabbage please. I hope there's bacon in it." Bleek watched her bemused. He was expecting her to ask for a salad with fruit or something. "Also, if there is cake or pie I want some with my meal and water. Thank you." Bleek nodded at the man who knew Bleek wanted a medium rare t-bone, baked potato and greens.

"Do they eat like this everyday?" Anastasia asked Bleek. Mena had disappeared. She would learn Mena was a quiet presence, only being seen as needed at her preference.

"Three times a day. Breakfast is at seven, lunch at one and supper at seven Monday through Friday. Sunday is a buffet. Juan, who you just met, yes Juan though he's Vietnamese is the lead cook. He's off on Saturdays and Sunday mornings. Be careful, you can get chubby eating here."

"Let my chubbiness be my concern." Anastasia said lightly, looking around. The men were eating, laughing and talking. Bleek watched her.

"I wasn't insinuating you are chubby."

In fact you're too damn fine. He thought.

"And I didn't say you did. Clearly spending your day with men has given you license to say what you wish and I'm sure being the boss doesn't hurt. Just be assured, Anastasia can hold her own." Roger strode to the table, sitting across from Anastasia.

"How's it going?" He asked Anastasia.

"The *job* is going splendidly." She responded. Bleek's nose flared at the meant insinuation.

Juan walked in, placing a plate in front of her with a massive sandwich, a bowl of cabbage and a slice of poundcake covered with macerated strawberries. She quickly mouthed a prayer and dug into her food. Roger gave Bleek a look of smug knowing. Bleek had met his match.

"Good, I'm taking off. Melba has called me four times. In fifty years of marriage she's now claiming my time." Roger said jovially.

"Where are you from Anastasia?" Bleek asked after their plates were clean. She had eaten every bite with relish.

"I was born and raised in Gainesville. I went to undergrad there but went to Columbia law school. My parents are still in Gainesville, both retired educators. I live between here and there in my own little paradise. I own two acres and a little house." Her eyes lit up speaking of her home.

"You weren't interested in staying in New York City?" Blake asked, something almost disdainful in his voice.

"No, not that there's anything wrong with New York, I created great memories there but I'm a home girl. I was hired by Roger right after law school before going out on my own. Land has always intrigued me. I found out as a teen that acres of land in Jacksonville had been stolen from Black families and that spurred my interest. I have traveled the south trying to right wrongs. Roger had to push me to do this." Her eyes met Bleek's. She saw something that looked like interest, quickly flicker away.

"You're fascinating, Ms. Anastasia. Tomorrow, we will ride the periphery—on horseback." He said, scraping back his chair and hurrying from the room.

She's almost too damn good to be real. She's brilliant, knows her shit and mine too and with that face, body and hair is a walking fantasy. And she smells like heaven. And her damn mouth says whatever it wants while being luscious. He thought storming to find BB.

"Do you need anything else?" Juan asked.

"No thanks, everything was wonderful."

Anastasia strode back to her office, working until five. Bleek filtered through her mind as she worked. She found him exasperating but was intrigued by his forthrightness. She met many millionaires and near billionaires but nothing about him indicated how much he was truly worth. She found him arrogant but not at conceited which felt almost contradictory. In a glance she saw confident man who loved ranching, was good to his employees but didn't give a damn about being politically correct or impressing people.

Anastasia was in Bleek's thoughts as well.

In addition to being smart—beautiful and sure of herself, she's also saucy and filled with fire

—

CHAPTER TWO

Anastasia drove to her parents after leaving work. She promised Joel and Sage Wright she would see them more since she would work less hours. Her parents were both seventy and retired after more than forty years of work. Anastasia was their only child and doted upon though they were both concerned about her lack of a social life. Sage hadn't been thrilled about her daughter working with a bunch of cowboys either. Cowboys in her mind was a bunch of wild, rowdy cave men. Joel had jokingly told her she was judging them wrongly, especially the cowboys of Blackmon Ranch. Sage wasn't convinced.

"Hey." Anastasia yelled, walking into the comfort of the home she grew up in. She placed her keys in a bowl by the door and kicked off her shoes. She knew they were in the kitchen, the center of their family life. Sage was on her feet when her daughter walked in.

Sage hugged her daughter, looking her over as if for damages.

"Your mama is looking for bruises from the buckaroos." Joel said humorously, hugging his daughter. Sage glared at him over Anastasia's shoulder.

"She needs to see Blackmon Ranch, it's like heaven on earth and the cowboys were all mannerable except the head cowboy, Bleek Blackmon, he's rude as can be. He's got great people around him. Even the food is amazing." Anastasia said, grinning at her dad's teasing and her mom's protectiveness.

"She does need to pay it a visit, there isn't even a saloon or shootouts." Joel said humorously. "I've been to a couple of events out there. It's definitely a ranch but it's not your run of the mill ranch. That young brother is so paid, the white folks and Arabs left him alone when acquiring land. They didn't even approach him. The word is he hired some of their trainers for them. He doesn't say much but he rides a horse and carries a big gun." Sage rolled her eyes. Joel loved teasing her.

"What did you eat?" Sage asked, changing the subject.

"For lunch I had a ribeye sandwich, cabbage and strawberry cake. It was delicious. There was all kinds of food. About four-thirty, Juan, the cook brought me a little black cooler with the company's logo on it. Inside was half a roasted chicken, garlic green beans, cornbread and more cake. Plus, a gallon of tea. It's a class operation."
Joel beamed but Sage looked unimpressed.

"I guess you don't need dinner then." Sage said.

"Of course I do. That's for later." Anastasia knew Sage had prepped her idea of a meal which was a salad with lean meats and lots of vegetables. Sage had been a size ten her entire adult life. Anastasia was taller and curvier but stayed fit with yoga every morning from six to seven and dance three times a week, she also walked a lot.

"I'm glad you didn't go to work for the others. They have raped the land, took folk's inheritance and selling million dollar homes. My buddy Jerry got seventy-thousand for his two acres. Now a two million dollar home is on that property. Even with the buildout that made them over a million and a half in profit." Joel said.

"I know dad but two years ago thirty five thousand an acre was unprecedented, the land then was worth about eight thousand an acre and that was considered great. I got my clients more than seventy an acre but your buddy Jerry, trusted them more than me." Joel couldn't argue with that. He tried convincing Jake but he wasn't willing to pay, in his worlds, for what he could do himself. Even with Anastasia's ten percent fee, he would have gotten almost a hundred and thirty thousand rather than seventy. But Jerry trusted men and white people more.

"Jerry's a fool but he learned." Sage said. Joel didn't respond. He had walked into that one. Jerry was old school and stubborn but every time he saw him nowadays he spoke with regret. Anastasia's most recent clients who held out initially had gotten even more with other benefits thrown in. Once she signed on to work for Blackmon she stopped taking on new clients for the other properties.

¥¥¥¥¥

During dinner Bleek sat with Frederick. In addition to being the lead horse trainer they were friends. He wooed Frederick from a top ranch in Montana ten years earlier. He relied on Frederick for honesty.

"Ms. Anastasia is one gorgeous woman." Frederick said. He was watching his friend who looked rakish and relaxed with his hat tipped back on his head.

"If you like that type." Bleek muttered.

Frederick's boisterous laughter rang out. He was laughing in his friend's face. Bleek's nose flared.

"Most red blooded straight men in the world like that type my brother. Beautiful face, body like a goddess and she looked you straight in your face and spoke her mind, you being her boss be damned. If I were a marrying man I would tip my hat. But Cheryl won't let me get another wife. Nathaniel and the other men confirmed it." Bleek did not take the bait. He had wasted too much time thinking of the damn woman already.

"You brothers act like the woman is the mother Mary, you just met her."

"All I know is if the mother was that fine, I understand why Joseph married her, knowing it wasn't his baby she was carrying." Bleek finally laughed. Frederick was a damn fool.

"Man, you need to take your ass home to your wife and that brood of yours."

"Oh, I will. But remember this, Nathaniel is a woman magnet. He doesn't have your money but women love that cowboy. Maybe even the good counselor would like to save a horse and ride a young cowboy. At twenty-nine, Nathaniel is a prime stallion." Bleek's eyes narrowed. "Speaking of stallions, I got a nice horse for Ms. Anastasia. He's ready to ride." Frederick tipped his hat before leaving the canteen. Bleek frowned at his roasted chicken and was no longer hungry. *Should've stuck with steak.*

"Hello Bleek." A sultry voice said. Bleek glanced at the woman standing at the table a platter of salad in her hands. She was Gloss Stewart, his PR lead and a woman he enjoyed a couple of sexual encounters with a couple of years ago. She was a good looking woman in her mid-forties who was always immaculately attired with never a hair out of place and her makeup a perfect mask. *Did Anastasia have on makeup, her lips were red…* Bleek wondered.

"Have a seat Gloss. How's the new campaign going?"

Gloss sat and dressed her salad with oil and vinegar before answering.

"It's going great but I need you on a horse for a photo Bleek. You promised." She whined. He had promised but despised promoting himself. He had a brand with his name on it but to date used actors in his ads. The horse he gave Anastasia was one of the horses they were showing. He had several for sale and him on one would probably bring in even better offers and the offers were great. An idea popped in his head.

"I'll give you two hours in the morning at ten. Have your photo shoot set up near the west stables by nine." He said. Gloss beamed and started picking over her salad. "Don't you want chicken or a steak? That looks unsatisfying." She made a face and placed her fork on the table. Her amber colored eyes met his.

"I have to stay fit. Perhaps one day I'll find my king."

"Perhaps you will, I'll see you at nine." He said.
She watched him stop and talk to his men on the way out. She was still carrying a torch for him but Bleek made it blatantly clear with everyone he was not the marrying kind. Not only that but his mother wanted grand babies and Gloss was past that occurring. Gloss raised her hand and Juan appeared at her table.

"Juan, could I please have a chicken breast with the wing attached." She asked.

"Roasted or fried?"

"You might as well fry it. I'll take bourbon as well."

Bleek took his third ride around the property before going to his cabin on the edge of the property away from everyone. His cabin was three thousand square feet, a modest home some thought for a man of his stature and means. In non-ranch assets, he was worth nine figures. But in his heart he was a simple man who loved ranching, riding, great food, excellent bourbon and message rappers like Kendrick Lamar, though country and reggae music flowed in his veins. He quietly donated millions annually to agencies serving minority youth, specifically Black youth. If he admitted it, he would say he was lonely but he wasn't there.

CHAPTER THREE

Mena handed Anastasia riding clothes and boots when she arrived. Beautiful well-made clothing and beautiful chocolate boots. Anastasia fingered the fine materials, impressed with them. They had discreet *Bleek Brand* labels. *The man has a brand.* Anastasia thought. *A brand he never mentioned and it was aside from Blackmon Ranch. It's hard to call him humble but he is— on this.*

"You're riding with Bleek in an hour. A car will take you there. It's too far to walk." Anastasia didn't question her. She understood, riding and being readily available was part of her excellent package.

"Fuck." Bleek muttered when Anastasia stepped out of the car driven by Frederick at nine-thirty. She looked like a luxury ad for cowgirl attire. *His* cowgirl attire. Everything hugged her form and she strode towards him confidently. Her hair was twisted and pinned up.

"What's all this?" Anastasia asked Bleek about the photo crew. She looked at everything except how damn chocolate and fine the man was. He was a jerk but too handsome.

"We, you and me are posing for a new ad. That chestnut beauty is all yours." He said, pointing to a gorgeous horse near BB. Anastasia's mouth flew opened as she hurried to the horse. She gently touched him, rubbing him firmly. Bleek watched the horse acknowledge her touch.

She's a damn horse whispering witch. He thought. His groin tightened watching her. He quickly turned away to find Gloss standing behind him in jeans and a satin shirt, a pink hat sitting jauntily on her hair.

"Who is *that*? She asked. Bleek turned to where she was pointing. Anastasia was on the horse, she had released her hair from the bun and huge, thick hair swirled around her shoulders. Bleek cleared his throat.

"That's Anastasia Wright, my new lead attorney. I figured since we are being more progressive, I need a cowgirl and she looks—she's perfect. Don't you agree?" Gloss pursed her lips together and sashayed over to the crew. Bleek strode over and jumped on BB.

"What's her name?" He asked Anastasia. Her eyes widened.

"I can name her?"

"She's yours."

"In that case she's Mocha. What's your horse's name?"

"This is BB, Bleek's Baby." He said. "Let's do this."

He started galloping and Anastasia followed him, grateful for years of lessons. She loved riding. The cameras started snapping. For two hours there were photos of them posed on the horses, others of them riding, Anastasia's hair flying behind her with a look of pure joy on her face and Bleek watching her as he rode behind her or beside her. There were a couple of them side by side, Bleek staring at her. She was smiling and staring ahead.

After the shoot, Bleek and BB lead them to the stalls, galloping slowly. Bleek got off to assist Anastasia but Nathaniel stepped in offering his assistance. For a fleeting second, Bleek thought of punching him. He quickly gathered himself and looked around. He caught Frederick's knowing look. Bleek glanced back at Anastasia who was smiling up at Nathaniel.

Gloss strode up and stood next to Bleek.

"She's quite something. Perhaps another conquest for Nathaniel." Bleek ignored the bait. "We should have taken photos of them."

"Ms. Wright." Bleek said. Anastasia turned to face him, her face glowing. She made her way over to where he stood.

"Mr. Blackmon." She said.

"This is Gloss Stewart, she's our public relations person. Gloss, this is Anastasia Wright, my—our lead counselor." Anastasia offered her hand to Gloss who shook it limply. "Ms. Wright, let's catch Frederick back to the canteen."

He walked towards the parked car, Anastasia striding beside him. He opened the door for Anastasia to get in front with Frederick, Bleek climbed in the back. Nathaniel, Gloss and several workers looked on in shock. They had never seen Bleek in the backseat even when Marie was in the car with a driver.

"Ah…" Nathaniel said. *Boss man likes her.*

Gloss rolled her eyes, storming off to her car.

"That was so fun." Anastasia said, scooping up her hair and expertly tucking it in a bun. Bleek stared out the window but the scent of what smelled like fresh flowers assaulted his senses. He was as hard as steel.

"You're a good rider Ms. Anastasia." Frederick said.

"I'm a little rusty but it all came back. My dad taught me and I took lessons. I might need to get me a horse, I have room on my property."

"Mocha is yours." Bleek said. She swirled in her seat to face him.

"Like mine, mine?" She asked her voice shocked.

"Yes but you can't move him yet." He hadn't turned from staring out the window. Frederick glanced in the rear view mirror. His boss' face was unreadable.

"Thank you." She said. *He's such a paradox, gruff as hell but generous.*

Anastasia chose a burger and salad for lunch with cake. Bleek had the same meal as the day before. They didn't talk during the meal but it felt less awkward somehow.

"You're a good rider, Ms. Anastasia. You will be compensated for the photo shoot, that was above and beyond your duties." Bleek said after the plates were removed.

"Thanks but I'm good. I was on the clock."

"There's no clock for you. When you work outside of your duties you get compensated." Anastasia shrugged.

"It's your dime sir. I'm going to get to work." She grabbed her extra dessert Juan provided before leaving.

He's as changeable as a chameleon.
Anastasia thought.

I'm riding in backseats, ready to fistfight my dude and giving away my damn horses. Over a woman I haven't known a full day. I need to get my ass together. Bleek mused watching her.

He sent a message to his managers including Anastasia he wouldn't be available the rest of the week. It was Tuesday. In addition to horses he loved motorcycles. He had a beach house on Tampa Bay. He needed to fish and unwind. He hadn't gone since losing his father, that was their thing. At least twice annually he and Bleek Jr. went to the house and fished for hours. Sometimes they didn't talk much. He missed his dad.

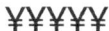

Right before five Anastasia heard a knock on her door. Gloss walked in. She had changed into a dress.

"How can I assist you?" Anastasia asked.

"I'm simply making the rounds. It's strange not having Roger in this office, he was Bleek's first employee, so he got the best office. You're making history, Blackmon's first female lead attorney, with the best office."

The office was spacious with a beautiful view of the property. Roger had gotten it decorated in neutral tones for his replacement.

"Which means it's past time, I'll say. Roger is my mentor and former employer. Are you the first *woman* public relations person and where is your office?" Gloss' perfect brow lifted.

"I'm not sure. Perhaps I'm historical as well." She didn't answer the office part, she didn't have an on site office. She was contracted.

"Perhaps. I have a call before leaving if you will excuse me." Anastasia said and picked up the phone. She did not do drama and everything about Gloss oozed drama. She also hadn't missed how the woman looked at Bleek.

She's quite snippy. Gloss thought as she made her way to Frederick's office. He was rarely in it but near the end of the day he sometimes was. She was infuriated and needed to vent.

"What's up Gloss?" Frederick said as she walked in and sat in the chair across from his desk.

"What's up with your boss and the debutante?" She asked.

"I have no idea what you mean."

"Okay, your boss is riding with someone other than you or the other cowboys, he invited her to a photoshoot, he wanted to chop Nathaniel's throat for assisting her, he rode in the backseat for her and now he's just gone. Something is up."

"Gloss, if you want to know anything about Bleek you have to ask him. But I'll say this, she's a brilliant attorney and the staff responds to her because she's straightforward and kind to everyone. She treats Bleek and Juan the same and it seems people respond to her energy."

His words did nothing to soothe Gloss' ruffled feathers. She felt dismissed by the newcomer and that annoyed her. Not as much as watching Bleek respond to her but close enough.

¥¥¥¥¥¥

Anastasia filled her tub with bath salts. Horse riding had used some under utilized muscles. She thought about the day and noted that on horseback Bleek looked free and almost happy. She also thought of the cast of characters she met over the past two days, Frederick was good people, Nathaniel too but full of his own attractiveness and Gloss had either been with Bleek or wanted to be. Anastasia's plan was to do her job and enjoy the amazing perks. The money was astounding, the food delicious and free— Juan sent her another meal to take home and she had her own horse, Mocha. She picked up the glass of wine she sat on the side and toasted her new job.

¥¥¥¥¥¥

Bleek sped across the state to Tampa. He hadn't packed. He had clothes at the cabin and his poles. He loved the anonymity of being a rancher. No one noticed him, he was just a brother on a Harley when he left the ranch and blended in. Today had been the first photo shoot he allowed.

How will that affect my ability to maneuver unknown? He wondered. *What the hell was I thinking?*

¥¥¥¥¥

Gloss and Marie checked the early images from the shoot. It would be weeks before the ads were out but Marie loved early looks. She wanted the ad to feature the shots with Bleek *and* Anastasia. Gloss didn't agree.

"If this is about promoting the ranch and *Bleek Brand* it should be just Bleek. No one even knows her." Gloss argued. Marie didn't look up, she was peering closely at every photo.

"A lot of folks know her—just not like this and the not being known like this is great for everything we represent. She's brilliant, successful and beautiful. More importantly she is a natural on horses. She's now part of the brand, my dear." Marie pulled off her spectacles and looked directly at Gloss.

"Surely, you understand how important having a woman's face can be for all of this." Marie waved her had around. "Surely."

Gloss knew once Marie said surely, everything else was moot at that point. Gloss also knew she couldn't go to Bleek. He gave Marie and his leaders full autonomy on making decisions. She didn't say anything more but would try later with Marie before the ads released.

"Gloss..." Marie said. The younger woman looked up from her computer. "Anastasia Wright is here to stay. I knew that the minute she arrived. Make your peace with it."

CHAPTER FOUR

After four days of fishing and sleeping, Bleek was home. He usually slept four hours a night but at the beach house he got in eight. But first he had to see Marie before going in to work. Marie lived on the far side of the property in the home his grandfather built. It was a great distance from Bleek's home to hers. He got dressed in jeans, a gray button down and boots. Atop his head was a gray leather cowboy hat.

Marie was in the huge kitchen when he arrived sipping coffee. She could make one cup last all day. Bleek kissed her forehead and washed his hands. He knew there was a plate of food for him in the warmer. Marie ate within half hour of waking. He grabbed the plate with fried pork chops, sautéed apples and homemade bread and sat across from his mother. Her eyes took in her handsome son. His hat was on a table near the door allowing her to see his hair which was a couple inches long and thick, nappy curls like hers.

Everything else in his looks was all his father and grandfather.

"How was the break and what inspired it?" Marie asked. She always got to the point. Bleek pointedly bit into his pork chop, chewing slowly before responding.

"This is a good pork chop. I enjoyed my break. I did a lot of fishing, in fact I shipped three coolers of redfish and speckled trout to the canteen yesterday before I rode out. As for inspiration I needed to just be Bleek a few days, where no one knew me or wanted anything—and I slept."

"Good for you. I saw Gloss Friday."

"Did you?"

He bit another piece of the crisp, perfectly seasoned meat.

"I did. She said you had Anastasia with you on the photo shoot. I think it's a great idea but what inspired it?"

"Anastasia did. She's a good, strong rider and she looks happy riding. Of course I learned that. You haven't seen the photos?"
Marie got final approval in on all public relations regarding the ranch. She had of course and approved them but wasn't telling Bleek until it was a done deal.

"It's great she loves horses. She also seems to love the work, the place and the cowboys like her. It's only been a week but Ms. Anastasia Wright is part of Blackmon Ranch."

Hearing that felt too pleasing to Bleek but his face showed nothing. His plan going forward was to treat Anastasia the same as his other employees.

"Don't lose her Bleek."

"Lose her? What does that mean?"

"It means you're attracted to her and you tend to push away people who get too close to that heart of yours. You haven't been involved with anyone in years other than the Gloss' of the world and we all know that's sexual maintenance. Son, it's okay to be attracted and to even do something about it. According to Roger, all she does is work."

"Seems you and Roger got it all figured out. Is that why he hired her?" Bleek wanted to bite back the words as soon as he said them. Marie stared at him like she didn't know him.

"Don't be an ass Bleek Blackmon and insult that woman or Roger. She's brilliant, capable and I'm sure she can pick or choose from any man in this state." Bleek leaned back in his chair, peering at Marie from under hooded eyes.

"That was—being an ass. Even if I thought that initially I know better. She's all you say but I'm not looking for a woman. Can I finish my food? I need to go to work."

"Yes sir Massa Blackmon." Marie said sarcastically. Bleek focused on his food.

¥¥¥¥¥¥

Anastasia felt in groove with her job after a week of working. She contacted current clients and worked with those who wanted to do business with the ranch, which was international. Robert, the accountant a very precise man invited her to his meetings bringing her up to speed on the financial aspect of the ranch. Anastasia was astonished the ranch had no mortgages or debt and Bleek was sole owner and operator. She had thought, *That's why no one messed with him or his property. The man is solvent and owns himself.* Robert made sure she knew that all occurred under the past fifteen years of Bleek's leadership. His cattle and horses sold internationally and he had several brands such as saddles, cowboy gear and other ranch products that sold worldwide. In addition to that he had horse trainers in Kentucky, Montana, Texas and Brazil.

Every day since getting Mocha, she rode him the first hour she was on the property before working. Her office had a bathroom with a closet. There was also a room with a bed.

At noon Anastasia walked into the canteen. The first person she saw was Bleek. He was standing at a table talking to Frederick and several of the men. She spoke to everyone and strode past him to the table she always sat at. Bleek tried not to but he turned to watch her. Juan was immediately at her side, taking her order and smiling. Juan never smiled. Anastasia returned his smile.

"She's got Juan." Nathaniel said, watching Bleek. Frederick was also observing Bleek who hadn't turned back to their conversation. Anastasia glanced at Bleek and he quickly looked away.

"What time are the kids arriving?" Bleek asked.

Quarterly he opened the ranch, allowing interested kids to come in to ride and learn about the business of raising horses and cattle.

"At two-thirty. There are thirty including seven girls. They are here until five thirty."

"Cool, I'm riding with them." He said before walking across the room to where Anastasia sat. He stood over her, forcing her to look up.

"How are you? Has everyone treated you well?" He asked. She looked up, her eyes cool but her beauty struck him in the throat. Her hair was back in a thick braid, her lips were covered with a sheen but no color and her skin was like milk chocolate velvet.

"I'm well and your staff is wonderful. Are you sitting or standing over me?" Bleek pulled out a chair and sat across from her.

"The high school is bringing in thirty students for a tour and ride from two- thirty to four-thirty. From four-thirty to five-thirty they will eat in here. If you have time please join us, there are seven young women."

"It's on my schedule." She said noncommittally. Bleek heard coolness in her voice, a professional distant tone. He didn't like it though he decided to avoid her but there he was unable to and in his feelings.

Juan walked in with a plate that held a perfectly fried redfish, bread and another with salad that he placed in front of Anastasia.

"Ma'am, Mr. Bleek caught the fish himself." Juan said. "Boss, you want the usual or fish?"

"I'll have a couple of the fish." Bleek said still watching Anastasia.

Bleek watched Anastasia pepper her fish with hot sauce and then pinch off bread and fish and pop it in her mouth. Her eyes closed with delight as she chewed. *She's so free—and too sexy for her own good. She has no idea of the affect she has on—people.*

"That's so good. Reminds me of Friday night fish fries." Her tone changed to more conversational. *Maybe the woman was hungry.* Bleek thought feeling silly.

"Ms. Anastasia you are kind of country."

"I'll be that. Please call me Anastasia, Bleek."

The way she said his name made his dick hard. He pushed his chair further under the table.

"Anastasia, it is."

Juan brought Bleek's food and they ate quietly. After Anastasia's plate was clean, Bleek asked, "no dessert?"

"Not yet. Juan said there will be ice cream sundaes with the kids meal, I'm waiting for that. I have a call." She said and excused herself.

She's everything mom said and more. Bleek thought. *Which makes her dangerous— to my peace.*

Marie was right, he hadn't dated anyone seriously since his father turned over the ranch to him at twenty-five and his dad was sixty-five. He poured all of his blood and sweat into growing the brand and widening their reach. He attended most functions alone and there were women always willing to grace his bed. Not just because he was handsome and wealthy but because he brought pleasure. Pleasure that made them crave him long after the sex ended. It had been a long time since any sexual maintenance occurred.

¥¥¥¥¥

When Bleek arrived at the stables, Anastasia was there with the kids, teachers and Nathaniel. He looked around for Frederick who usually drove her. There was almost three miles from her office to the west stables.

"Where's Frederick?" Bleek asked.

"He had to get the horses ready sir, I drove Ms. Anastasia." Nathaniel answered. He noted a slight flare to Bleek's nose.

"It's time to assign her a truck." Bleek said gruffly. "She's a rancher now." Nathaniel nodded. He understood the assignment and more.

Anastasia was talking to the kids and allowing them to touch Mocha. The girls, two black, two Asian and three white looked enamored with Mocha and Anastasia who was in full cowgirl regalia down to chaps that hugged her thighs like a glove.

"Saddle up." Bleek said once Frederick brought out the horses. The kids were excited. "And be careful." He said climbing on BB.

Nathaniel spoke to Frederick as everyone got on the horses.

"Bleek wants a truck assigned to Ms. Anastasia. Am I missing something?" Nathaniel asked.

"Get her the truck, in time you'll see if you're missing anything. Give her the new limited longhorn."

"I'll get it done."

"Nate—stay away from her."

"I already know but *you* asked me to drive her."

"Now I'm asking this."

¥¥¥¥¥

The canteen was loud and boisterous with twenty excited teens who were given a tour by Bleek and allowed to ride prize horses. Juan prepared his version of pizza which was pulled pork on homemade dough with cheese and homemade tomato sauce. There was also burgers, hot dogs and bowls of fruit salad in addition to an ice cream sundae station he set up. The kids were laughing and talking with Anastasia and several of the older cowboys in their midst were telling tales. Bleek leaned against the bar watching everyone, Frederick at his side.

"I forget how fun this is. It's great to see Black kids. There were ten black boys and the two girls. Years ago no black kids signed up."

"I could see you enjoying yourself. It's a good look, rich niggas have fun too." Laughter poured out of Bleek's throat causing everyone to look his way. Anastasia was astonished at the transformation of his face. He was a gorgeous man but laughter elevated his look. When his hat slid off and he caught it and she saw his hair, her heart raced. It looked thick and strong and there was enough to hide your hands in. Heat filled her. Bleek felt her eyes and glanced her way, the smile still on his face. She returned the smile and his broadened as he set the hat back on his head, jauntily.

She just saw his ass, really saw his ass for the first time. Frederick thought. *She looks as struck as he did last week when she pulled her hair down and mounted Mocha. It's over for both of them.*

One of the kids called Anastasia's name. She turned to face them breaking the stare. Bleek continued to look her way, his eyes not wavering.

Save A Horse, Ride A Cowboy came through the speakers and the girls jumped up grabbing Anastasia's hands, pulling her to the floor. They showed her a quick two-step which for some reason made her laugh.

"If for one minute y'all think I can't dance to country music, I got news for you. I just need proper music. DJ give me a beat." She yelled.

The Girl's Gone Wild by Travis Tritt came on and Anastasia broke loose, dancing to the beat, every step and sway in tune. It was the sways that had Bleek standing straight with his hands in his pocket. Most of the kids joined in and a couple of the cowboys. Nathaniel chose that moment to enter the room.

"Come on Nate, I know you can dance," Anastasia yelled. Nate hesitated but couldn't resist the call.

She called him Nate." Bleek thought.

After a couple of minutes of watching them dance and laugh together, Bleek made his way across the floor without thinking and took her hand pulling her away, ignoring Nathaniel. She went with him, without question. The music changed to *Live Like You Were Dying* by Tim McGraw. They danced perfectly in sync for the duration of that song with everyone clapping them on. Even the kids applauded. After the second song, Bleek released her hand and left the building.

"What the hell just happened?" Nathaniel asked Frederick.

"I think from what I saw Bleek Blackmon is laying claim to Anastasia Wright and he doesn't even know he's doing it. I also think Ms. Anastasia thinks you're fun but she's not looking at you the way she looked at him." Frederick said.

"Hell, I might be a simple cattleman but I ain't blind. I need to talk to him." Frederick tried to stop him but Nathaniel walked outside where Bleek was posted up drinking a bottle of water.

"Can we talk?" Nathaniel asked. Bleek gave him a dark look but said, "You got the floor."

"This job is the best thing that happened to me. I'm not trying to cross you over anything."

Bleek drained his water bottle, crushed it in his hand and tossed it in the trash bin, several yards away.

"Be more specific Nathaniel, we are men out here."

"I find Ms. Anastasia attractive but once I sensed you do as well, I stay in my lane. I didn't choose to drive her today, I was asked, I didn't ask her to dance, she asked me. I know my reputation with women but I'm not on that with her. I'm definitely not on that with you."

"Duly noted. You're one of my best managers, as long as you manage things we are good. But—she's—stay away from her." Bleek said

his dark intense glance fully on Nathaniel.
Nathaniel nodded in understanding.
"Now let's get those kids on the bus and give me the key to her truck."

"Yes sir." Nathaniel offered Bleek his hand which he shook firmly. He then gave him the keys and went to round up the kids. Frederick walked out as Nathaniel walked in.

"Everything good?" Frederick asked Bleek.

"Not everything but Nathaniel and I are."

Anastasia walked out with the kids past Bleek and watched them load on the buses. All the girls hugged her. When the bus pulled off, Bleek said, "If you have time, we are going on a tour."

"I have time." She responded softly. He started walking and she followed him to a beautiful black truck. He helped her get in.

"This truck is assigned to you. We only drive trucks, Ram trucks specifically on the property. There are thousands of acres and you can ride or drive. I'm going to drive you around the periphery. There are stables on the east and west of the property. The family home is far east and my home far west. In the middle is the cattle land that stretches beyond where you can see. There are twenty, two men apartments out there for the workers and there's a traditional bunkhouse as well but modern. The only managers that live onsite are Nathaniel and Juan. Juan worked for my dad. There are seventy day workers who drive in daily and of course contractors such as Gloss and others."

Anastasia listened as he drove, pointing out different areas. She was in awe by the sheer size of everything. Once they reached where the cattle were, she gasped. There was prime cattle beyond what the eye could see and men working with them.

"This is so impressive." She said. "Bleek, you are so blessed to own this and for generations. I'm thrilled with my two acres but this is astonishing." He peered at her checking everything and he saw the excitement on her face. "I love this place, I'm honored to work here."

Bleek was surprised by the lump that filled his throat. No woman had ever shown such excitement for what the place was about. The ones he met only saw what the land brought in terms of money and his net worth.

"It's home." He said humbly. "I'm going to end the tour here but we will do this again to cover all of it."

He drove her back to the office and placed the keys in her hands.

"I have a meeting with the Europeans at nine tomorrow. I'll pick you up here at eight-fifteen." His stare was direct, causing her to feel a bit unnerved. He usually didn't quite meet her gaze.

"The Europeans?"

"Yes, white folks largely who I call the Europeans because many are. A few rich Brazilians and Arabs as well. It's mostly pomp and circumstance. You'll see."

"I'll be ready." She said. He tipped his hat and walked into the darkening evening. She watched him until he disappeared.

He's the most fascinating man. She thought.

On the table in her office was her nightly food box from Juan.

Blackmon Ranch is good to its people.

Bleek walked more than an hour before getting in his truck, just like the one he gave Anastasia. His phone buzzed and he was surprised to see Anastasia's office number.

"Bleek."

"Can I please, please drive my truck home."
She asked, bringing a smile to his face.

"It's yours to drive as you wish. Enjoy it."

"Thanks Bleek." She said, hanging up gently.

Driving home she felt like a badass. She
would never have bought a truck for herself
or imagined a truck could feel so luxurious.
*Bleek Blackmon is first class all day and all
the way.* She thought.

CHAPTER FIVE

At eight-fifteen Bleek knocked on Anastasia's office door. Her eyes widened at the sight of him. He was wearing a charcoal colored suit of the finest materials and fit, with a pale blue shirt and lariat tie. His hat was leather and the color of smoke.

In turn his gaze took her in. Her attire was a snug-fitting black dress that stopped just above her knees. Around her neck were ropes of azure colored pearls with matching earrings and her hair was up and her makeup natural but her lips were perfectly red. Bleek cleared his throat before speaking.

"You clean up well Anastasia Wright."

"You do as well Bleek Blackmon."

She grabbed her leather bag and walked out the door around him. A masculine scent with a hint of tobacco essence assaulted her senses as she passed him.

He followed her to the waiting car, this time a V Series Black-wing Cadillac. He opened the door, assisting her in before getting in on the driver's side and pulling away from the curb.

Robert, Frederick and Nathaniel watched them from a distance.

"They look like King and Queen of everything." Nathaniel said. "It's a done deal." The other men nodded in agreement.

"You're right and he doesn't even know it. He's sprung. She's the kind of woman where he will have to make his move. She won't chase him or make herself available without that." Frederick said.

"As it should be." Robert said. "No one wants the easy ones, if they do, not forever. That one is forever."

¥¥¥¥¥

"My truck drives great." Anastasia said. "Do you only purchase American vehicles?"

"Yes, Dodge Ram trucks and Cadillac cars. I like them, I don't have a problem with your cute little Benz."

"Cute little? You will not besmirch my baby. I saved two years to buy her, she's a big-bodied boo." Anastasia said rolling her neck. A huge smile covered Bleek's face. *She's funny.*

"The EQS series is nice, I stand corrected. I'm a traditionalist, my ancestors bought Rams and Cadillacs. I have no problems with big-bodied boos."

"I'm sure you don't." Anastasia responded.

Bleek chuckled at her tone and what he felt she meant.

"This crowd are the wealthiest ranchers in the world. They are entitled and might say anything. They tolerate me and invite me to everything. I go because I know they would prefer I didn't. I'm an anomaly to them, getting past being Black, it's mostly I don't try to be anything I'm not or fit in as anything other than Bleek Blackmon."

Those words resonated with her more than anything he said prior. She was no multimillionaire but she earned enough for many to think she should be different or run in certain crowds but that's not who she was. She suspected the same was true of Bleek. When he wasn't alone he was with the men who worked for him and she felt genuine friendship between him and Frederick and him and Juan. More importantly he respected all of them even with his gruffness. Most of her free time was spent resting these days or with her parents. Most of her friends were as busy as she was and dating was in the not too recent past.

"I can fully appreciate that."

¥¥¥¥¥

Once they were inside, Anastasia saw exactly what Bleek meant. There were lots of smiles that didn't meet eyes. Bleek stood out in stature and wealth at the top because whereas some had more land and livestock, he had no debt thus a much better bottom line. There was grudging respect and varied admiration. Anastasia noted there were lots of unattached young women floating about mostly white and blonde. The men as Bleek described were mostly white and older with a couple of Brazilians and young Arabs.

"Well, who have we here?" A booming, masculine voice yelled out. They turned to a modest-sized man in an oversized hat and florid red face. "Finally, Blackmon has a filly. You're a beauty too. He's usually running around with the help."

"Oops, it seems he's doing it again."
Anastasia said. "I'm the help too, Anastasia
Wright, Blackmon Ranch lead attorney, and
you are?" The man's face grew even redder
but he grinned showing all of his smoke
stained teeth.

"I'm Bill Stein, I own the biggest cattle ranch
in these parts." Bill said, seeming to puff out
his chest. Bleek said nothing, he was
watching Anastasia in action.

"Congratulations, Bill Stein. Mr. Blackmon,
I'm parched, I could use a drink." Anastasia
said, walking away. Bleek nodded at Bill and
followed her. There were a couple more
introductions of that kind before they found
their seats. One of the Arab men said to
another in Arabic, "I'll buy her." Bleek
responded in English, "She's not for sale."
The men walked away. Anastasia was
chatting with people who greeted her.

Several of the blonde women managed to
greet and touch Bleek in some way as they

passed. Bleek's table was front and center where they sat alone. They were offered drinks which they both declined.

The meeting mostly focused on current rules of law, the climate for breeding and selling, cattle mostly and there were presentations and speeches.

"Exciting stuff." Anastasia said after the meeting and they were in the car.

"It's not the least bit exciting but it goes with it. Are you hungry?" He asked surprising Anastasia.

"I could eat but I can wait until we reach the ranch."

"Even if I promise to get you fries with your hamburger?" Her mouth watered at the thought.

"It depends on the burger."

Bleek drove several miles and turned left. About a mile in he pulled up to a small black building with large letters reading Barns Burgers on the side. There were two picnic tables but a long line at the window. Bleek pulled into a parking space and got out and opened the door for her. For ten minutes no one came out but when they did, an older Black man with a pronounced limp and peaceful expression had two baskets with burgers and fries. Bleek stood to embrace him.

"Thanks Mr. B, this is my attorney, Anastasia Wright. Anastasia, this is Mr. Barns, the Barns in Barns Burgers."

"Nice to meetcha Ms. Wright. I been feeding this young man since he was nine or ten and his daddy bought him here. Now he's bringing pretty lady lawyers." Anastasia smiled at him.

"It's nice to meet you sir. Can I have hot sauce, please?"

A young woman walked out with a tray with water and condiments.

"This here is my granddaughter, she's slow but cheap labor. Y'all enjoy and you come back soon, Ms. Anastasia."

"Sure will."

She cut her burger, and took a bite. A moan of joy escaped her. It was perfect, firm bun, pickles, tomato, bacon and juicy beef. Bleek watched her chew, his gut tightening. "Lord, that's good. I thought Juan's burgers were delicious but this is it." She licked a bit of tomato off her lip and Bleek looked away.

"Mr. B is eighty-one, same age as my dad. They were best friends in high school but after graduation in 1959, he went to the military and my dad became a rancher. Four years later Mr. B. got out with a disability. Vietnam was cranking up. The plan was for him to work on the ranch but that was out due to the limp, so my dad helped him get this place. He's been here since 1965. Until five years ago he only sold burgers and fries but his son convinced him chicken wings would sell even better. Now he only sells wings, burgers and fries. This place sent two kids and a grandchild to college and built a home. Anastasia, these are my people, nothing changes that. That's why the Europeans don't dig me and a lot of fancy Black folks either. I'm a cowboy, the rest of this is legacy."

Anastasia drank in his words. Feeling the honesty of them and a bit of something else. She watched him polish off his burger and empty his bottle of water. He placed a bundle of bills in the basket.

"Time to work counselor."

The ride back to the ranch was quiet but comfortable. Bleek stole glances at Anastasia as she stared out the window, taking in the beautiful countryside. Most of the city and surrounding areas had no idea of what was several miles from their front door.

After dropping Anastasia at her office Bleek went to change. The word legacy pounded in his brain. His mom's words about having someone to leave it all to felt real. Too real.

CHAPTER SIX

For more than three weeks Anastasia only saw Bleek in passing. They were having the annual horse sale and he flew overseas a couple of times for horse business. She was busy as well because the legalities of overseas sales and transfers were time consuming but the legal team working with her were stellar. One in particular, Leon Ambrose in his late forties worked harder than any of them. He was a divorced father and married to agricultural and equine law.

"Ms. Wright working with you has been a pleasure. Blackmon made the 'Wright' choice with you. Are you married?" Leon asked. Interest sparked in his eyes.

"I am not, what makes you ask?" Leon was a handsome man with charm to burn.

"I was thinking of inviting you for a meal or something."

"I'll take a rain check on the or something but let me treat you to a meal." She said, realizing she hadn't had a meal off the ranch since arriving. Or cooked a meal.

"I'll accept, no steak please." He said humorously. Every day in addition to other choices, the ranch, naturally, had steak. The best steak but Anastasia understood.

"You got it. Follow me."

Anastasia drove to a cozy Italian restaurant she had been meaning to try.

Once they ordered and settled in Anastasia found Leon charming and funny but beyond that had no interest. Since her burger with Bleek almost a month ago he filled her thoughts.

"Anastasia." Bleek's voice said behind her.

She turned to face him. He was standing with Robert at his side. He had been in Texas and

California the past week. He was suited and beautiful with hair growing on his chin but his eyes were tired but fully on her.

"Hey Bleek, welcome home."

Leon stood offering Bleek his hand which he shook but he was focused on Anastasia.

"I thought the least I could do is offer Leon a meal, he's worked hard this week." She said, her eyes searching Bleek's. He finally smiled a bit.

"That's the Blackmon Ranch way. And you are Blackmon Ranch." He said. "I'm going to grab a bite, I'll see you in the morning."

The you are Blackmon Ranch felt so intimate. It wasn't lost on Leon either. The energy between the two of them was palpable.

"Okay."

The remainder of the meal was anticlimactic. Anastasia felt rattled and annoyed for explaining to Bleek why she was there. *He's my boss, nothing else.*

"You better do something about it." Robert said once they were seated. Bleek picked up the menu knowing he was going to order oxtail lasagna. He held up his hand and asked for bourbon, two rocks.

"Maybe I will." Bleek finally said. He was facing the door and saw Anastasia and Leon get up to leave. She turned to look at him— she smiled and he grinned at her, relaxing. "Yea, maybe I will."

He didn't tell Robert they stopped because he saw her truck parked outside as they approached. The intent was to take Robert to his truck and grab food from the canteen. But he had to see her—and who she was with if anyone. Thoughts of her had invaded his sleep for weeks.

¥¥¥¥¥

Bleek dropped Robert off at his office and saw Anastasia's truck parked in her space. It was almost eight pm, more than an hour since she left the restaurant. He got out and strode to her office, knocking on the door.

"Come in." She said. He walked in and saw her gathering her things. It was Friday. "I knew Juan would leave me food, so I came back and started working…" she said but her words caught in her throat as Bleek walked closer to her and touched her face lightly. His hands were rough and felt too good on her skin.

"You're so damn beautiful woman. I tried ignoring you and whatever the hell you're doing to me." He said, his voice rough, his eyes narrowed. His rough thumb caressed her face, sending shockwaves of desire through her. She was unable to speak and her mouth was dry. She licked her lip and Bleek groaned deep in his throat and covered her mouth with his, sucking her tongue into his mouth. He groaned and she moaned as the kiss deepened. He kissed her until they were both breathless. He pulled away, looking down at her. She saw the hunger in his eyes and felt the hunger in her. She wanted to wrap her legs around his thigh and—ride.

"I'm going home Anastasia but tomorrow we are going on a drive. I'll pick you up at noon. I need—I will pick you up tomorrow."

"Do you know where I live?" Was all she could think to say, her body felt ignited.

"You're Blackmon Ranch Anastasia, of course I do. Get out of here and I'll see you tomorrow." She grabbed her purse and reached for her computer. "No work tomorrow or tonight—now go, I'll lock up."

She ran from the room. She wanted nothing more than to stay be kissed him until the sun came up.

Okay Bleek, you made your move. Don't fuck it up. He said to himself as he got in his truck.

¥¥¥¥¥

Anastasia saw a missed call on her phone once she was home. She didn't recognize the number but returned the call. Leon answered.

"Is everything okay?" She asked.

"No but I'm going to be bold and ask, "Are you involved with Bleek Blackmon?"

Anastasia certainly felt involved after the kiss earlier but that wasn't Leon's business.

"I find that an inappropriate question Leon." She answered.

"My apologies in that case. Don't blame a man for asking. You're a beautiful woman aside from your other attributes—of course I mean your legal mind and accomplishments. Take care." He said.

No one has asked me out in months, now I'm on. Anastasia mused as she undressed and filled her huge stand-alone tub with hot water. She was exhausted and planned to sleep until at least ten. After showering she crashed. The past two weeks she worked sixty hour weeks. Bleek frowned on that unless it was necessary. He felt if you couldn't get it done in forty hours he needed to hire more people. The past weeks were necessary.

Bleek paced his room like a panther. He showered and tried to watch the game but all he could think of was the soft skin on Anastasia's face, the way she looked at him and the taste of her. *She's so sweet—I'm losing my shit. I want her and I might even need her. I for damn sure don't want anyone else to have her. I need to check her interest, fully.*

CHAPTER SEVEN

By eleven, Anastasia was up, dressed with a packed bag, just in case and her hair was down but full curls from water and moisturizer. She was dressed in fitted knit pants, a long sleeved t-shirt, both black and short boots. She made a smoothie for breakfast in case they didn't stop for a meal. The door chimed at eleven-forty-five surprising her. Bleek was on time to a fault. She opened the door to Sage on her doorstep with a covered pan. *Oh hell.* She thought.

"You look mighty pretty on a Saturday morning Anastasia, you even have on shoes." Sage said, kissing the side of her daughter's face and stepping in around her. Anastasia took a deep breath and followed her mom to the kitchen. *Hopefully, she'll leave before Bleek arrives.* But Sage hopped up on a stool at the counter and placed the dish there.

"I cooked your favorite vegetable and shrimp lasagna. I know you've been craving home cooking, working all those hours. We haven't seen you in almost two weeks."

"Mom, that's not unusual when I'm busy. I eat very well each day. The ranch provides three meals daily."

"Umm, okay. That's a nice truck, the ranch provided that too?"

"Yes. I was about to head out. Thanks for the food." The lasagna was her favorite but she wanted Sage to leave. She didn't want questions about Bleek.

"Why do you look so skittish?"

"I don't." Anastasia said and sat down.

¥¥¥¥¥

She said this was her little house. Bleek observed pulling onto the property.

Anastasia's house was a large, one story structure surrounded by ancient trees. The walls of the home were brick and glass. *This house is classy like her.* The yard was beautiful grass and no flowers but with her schedule that made sense. He pulled up the long driveway and saw a Buick parked next to her truck. He got out and pressed the buzzer.

Inside Anastasia bolted from her chair but caught herself and slowed down. Sage followed her. She opened the door to Bleek with no hat, dressed in jeans and a white shirt with cuff links, looking like a wet dream. He grinned down at her, she returned the grin. Sage pushed around her.

"Hello, I'm Sage Wright, Anastasia's mother and I assume you're Bleek Blackmon." Bleek's smile broadened and he turned on the charm. Anastasia blinked, wondering who this Bleek was. He took Sage's hand in his and shook it firmly.

"I am Bleek, Mrs. Wright, it's a pleasure to finally meet you." Sage giggled like a schoolgirl.

"Clearly Anastasia's been hiding you. Are you working here today?" Sage asked. Anastasia rolled her eyes, Bleek noting that smiled even wider, every one of his perfect teeth showing.

"No ma'am. We are going on a little road trip." Sage looked from Bleek to her daughter who looked pained.

"Nice, I love a road trip. Have fun, Anastasia you're just full of surprises and secrets aren't you? But I do understand." Sage said before shaking her finger at Anastasia and leaving. They were still standing in the door.

"Come in."

Bleek followed her to the kitchen, checking out the spacious and elegant rooms.

"Your home is beautiful." Bleek said. "Nice property too."

"Thank you." Anastasia said, placing the casserole in the freezer and looking around before allowing her eyes to light on Bleek. He was watching her, intensely. "I bought the land a year after I started working. It took two years to build the house I wanted, I believe in paying as you build. I'm a no debt girl."

"That's impressive but I really need to get out of this house—Bleek said. He wanted to take her upstairs. "I'll be outside." He rushed out. Anastasia did another check and grabbed her bag before following him out. Bleek noted the bag meaning she was open to an overnight.

"I'm taking you to my west coast place. If you can stay overnight, I would be as— gentlemanly as possible. It has two bedrooms."

"I can—we will see on the gentleman thing." She said. Bleek adjusted in his seat.

"Your mom is a beauty."

"She is. I grew up wanting to look like her but alas I'm the image of Joel Wright."

"Your dad looks like a woman?"

"Sure does." She said saucily. "A six foot-two inch, two hundred sixty pound woman. Anastasia has two mommies."

"That mouth."

"Comes with the rest of me. What are we doing Bleek?"

"I'm hoping to get to know you. You know, I hope, that I'm attracted to you. I didn't want to be but from the day you walked in my office you shook me up and didn't seem impressed with my ass, at all. I realized how shook up I was every time I saw you with Nathaniel and last night with Leon." He admitted.

"I wasn't *with* either of them. Nathaniel is a fun flirt, only good for that. Leon asked me to dinner or drinks. I flipped it by inviting him, I have no interest in him. As for you—my initial thought was what an asshole. I still think you have lots of asshole tendencies but here we are anyway."

Bleek's booming laughter filled the truck.

"You do know it's okay, to filter what you say Anastasia."

"And get plowed over by you, that is not happening. I recall you saying day one, "This is a ranch Ms. Wright and we don't take time for the proper words and questions necessarily. I'm with that."

Bleek couldn't stop laughing for several minutes. *She can handle me. I'm the one who needs to step up.*

"What music do you like?" Bleek asked.

"My hip-hop faves are Kendrick, Pac and DMX. R and B is Ronald Isley bar none. For country it's Garth Brooks and blues Etta James. But I love music, period but those are my G.O.A.Ts."

"That's a hard list, especially the hip-hop. R and B for me is vintage, Marvin Gaye. Blues B.B. King and country I'm going with Tim McGraw but like you I'm a music lover. No Beyoncé or H. E. R.?"

"You stay with the stereotypical judgments but I can listen to both and enjoy them. Music isn't like I can't love Etta James and Beyoncé."

"Hardly judgmental though maybe some stereotypes because the few women I know from teens to older love Beyoncé and H.E.R. I like H.E.R. on her guitar and when Beyoncé does soldier I think of joining the military."

"Oh, okay then. Is it the music or the video esthetics?"

"Let me think because those esthetics will pull a brother in."

Anastasia snorted trying to control her laughter but it poured out.

"How many Bleeks are in there? I've seen grumpy Bleek, kind Bleek, all business Bleek and with my mom, lady-killer Bleek."

"Which one do you like?"

"Who said I like any of them?"

"You like something, you're in my truck with your overnight bag."

"Cocky mutha…"

"Wo! Ms. Anastasia, how many of you are there?"

"As many as necessary Mr. Bleek, don't be fooled by the law degree."

"I'm scared, I might have to turn around."

"I doubt that."

"And I'm cocky?"

"Yes."

Bleek pressed a button and Ronald Isley's beautiful voice filled the truck. Anastasia closed her eyes, listening. Bleek snuck glances, wanting to kiss her again…all over her body.

CHAPTER EIGHT

"We're here." Bleek said. Anastasia opened her eyes and sat up. The scene before her made her blink. They were in the driveway of a home that seemed to jut over the ocean. It was like seeing the Gulf of Mexico in 3D.

"This is stunning." She said, getting out. Bleek got out and held the door for her.

"It's where my dad and I got away. I bought it when I was thirty and he was almost seventy. We got ten years here. He was never sick. One night he told mom he was tired and went to bed. He was gone when she went to bed. I miss him but he lived a great life and what a way to go." She searched his face for sadness but there wasn't any she could see, just memories.

"How's your mom doing?"

"She seems good. Dad wasn't around a lot, even when he retired at sixty-five. He felt he needed to be part of every association. That was something we disagreed on. I go where I must, he wanted to be on every scene and was until about a year before he died. That's why the old heads don't understand me, they wanted another version of my dad. I loved and admired my dad more than any man but all that grinning and shaking hands wasn't me. He found it powerful to be accepted in white spaces, I understand that it's *perceived* power. I figured power was owning and growing the ranch beyond encroachment."

"That's generational. Your dad was born in 1940, you in 1981, that's technically two generations—in America."

"I know but I wasn't doing all that. It's worked out."

"That much is true. I really need to pee." She said.

Bleek locked the truck and went to to unlock the cabin. Anastasia rushed to the restroom, led by Bleek. He told her he was going to pull the truck closer and get their bags. After using the restroom, Anastasia washed her hands and face and pulled her hair back. She looked around the huge bathroom which was spartan, everything was white with white towels and washcloths. She walked through the hall to the way they came in. The living room was large overlooking the ocean. It held two large chairs, a table and not much else with beautiful rugs on the floor. It led into a modern kitchen where Bleek was unloading a cooler.

"Juan packed this cooler. There are premade sandwiches, fruit and a cake. In the other cooler that I unpacked there are steaks, shrimp, bread and salad fixings. Are you hungry?"

"I'm starving. I only had a smoothie."

Bleek grabbed two huge sandwiches wrapped in wax paper, grapes and bananas.

"We will get a proper meal later. Wait for me on the porch."

She walked outside and the view was even better. It was so close. She sat on one of the loungers pulled up to the balcony and leaned forward. The air was so clean. Bleek walked out, placing a platter in the table with two sandwiches and the fruit in a bowl.

"I think I'm going to marry Juan." Anastasia said after eating half of a chicken sandwich with tomato and garlic pickles.

"He's in love with you but I have to say Juan has worked for the family since I was a kid. I've never seen him with a woman. Every other year he returns to his country for a month. He doesn't discuss family. He's sixty-five and says he's going to die at that stove."

"You're good to your people."

"Are you my people Anastasia?"

"I hope so. Bleek, I'm sleepy."

"Of course you are. I'll be out here, it's around the corner from the bathroom you used."

She entered the room to fresh orchids on the table next to the bed, a box of pralines and a bottle of water. There was a white robe on the bed. She touched it. *Oh, it's cashmere.* The room was sparsely furnished but beautiful with the same view. There was also a bathroom with a shower, sink and toilet, all white. Her bag was in a chair. She was too tired to unpack but took a quick shower and wrapped the robe around her before getting on the bed. She was asleep in minutes.

¥¥¥¥¥

Three hours later Bleek decided he needed to check on Anastasia. He had showered and changed into sweats and T-shirt. He also readied the steak for the grill. He knocked on the door but didn't get an answer. He pushed the door open and stopped in his tracks. She was sprawled on her back, the robe open at the top and one her perfect breasts was on display, her nipple puckered. Her hair was spread over the pillow and her mouth was slightly open. His dick grew painfully hard.

Man stop being a peeper. Anastasia rolled over on her side and he backed out of the room. *Her nipples are—got-damn.* He hurried out to the balcony. It was cool with the sea breeze.

An hour later Anastasia walked outside. The robe was tied around her.

"I'm so sorry, I was tired."

"Open your robe." Bleek said.

It sounded almost like a demand. It turned her on. She opened the robe and let it puddle on the floor. Bleek's mouth watered at her beauty. She looked like a goddess. The best part was her stomach that looked soft and sweet—after those nipples. He moved closer and pulled her belly into his face and placed his tongue in her navel. Anastasia hissed. He held her and licked from her belly down to her bare mons. Her legs spread as she grew wet. He continued kissing her until his talented tongue touched her clitoris. She yelled with pleasure and tried to move but he held fast, lashing her with his tongue, making her thighs quiver. He pulled her closer, moving his tongue harder and faster until he felt her climax building. He sucked and she exploded over his tongue, her hands holding his hair, tight. He continued lavishing her.

"Bleek—you're killing me." She pled.

He stood suddenly and scooped her up, carrying her to the room. He somehow got out of his clothes and pushed inside her. A moan escaped her and he muttered something unintelligible as he lost himself inside her. Neither thought about protection. Bleek had always been diligent but he needed and had to feel all of her. He pressed her legs against her chest and went for everything he felt. She exploded, dragging his climax out of what felt like his gut.

"Anastasia." He said before kissing her fiercely. He hardened again and slowed down his love making, staring down at her. *I'm lost to her.* He thought as she met him grind for grind and thrust for thrust, her gaze of desire holding his.

"Damn." He said after his second climax.

"Double damn." Anastasia said.

"I—" Bleek started.

"Me too. We wanted this, hell I needed it."

"With me?"

"Hell yea, with you. I wouldn't be here if not with you." She said.

"I needed to know that Anastasia. I care—that you care. If that makes sense."

"It makes perfect sense."

She cuddled closer. He wrapped her in his arms and buried his face in her hair. There was so much he wanted to say that felt too damn soon. Her growling belly saved him.

"I have steak ready for the grill and salad."

"That sounds so good. Let's get dressed."

"In a minute." He said. He covered her mouth with his.

¥¥¥¥¥

Sage was in the kitchen a magazine spread out on the table.

"What's that?" Joel asked looking over her shoulder. Sage closed the magazine and pointed to the cover. On the cover of *International Horse Magazine* was a photo of Anastasia on a beautiful horse, a huge smile on her face with her hair flying; superimposed in the background was Bleek Blackmon on his horse, his eyes on her, his attraction unguarded.

"Did you know about this? That is something to see." Joel said.

"If you think this is something and it is, I've never seen her look more beautiful or alive but this morning I stopped by to take her some food. Ms. Anastasia was as jumpy as a cat with her hair down and this same man who is bigger and *much* better looking in person arrived." Joel's brow lifted. "He told me they were going on a day trip and she was in good hands. I guess so because his hands are big. Look through the magazine, she looks like the cowgirl of the year and he looks like a cowboy ought to."

"Sage, you are saying a lot."

"I sure am. That man is hot—and our baby girl is hotter. That is all this *proud* mama is saying. Whoo Lord."

Joel flipped through the magazine and was impressed by the fact half the spreads were of Anastasia and *her boss.*

"Sage, he's her boss *and* you didn't want her working with those wild cowboys if I remember correctly."

"First of all no one bosses Anastasia Wright and second of all, who cares now I've met him. My daughter who hasn't dated since Obama was president it seems is dating him. In addition to looking like that, the man is a zillionaire or something. Think of the beautiful babies. Anastasia is thirty-six!"

"Sage, you're jumping the gun. These are photos woman."

"Okay Joel. Mark my words, that's our son-in-law. And—it's not like he's any old cowboy."

Women. Joel thought.

¥¥¥¥¥

On the ranch, Marie was beaming. She chose the photos she wanted against Gloss' recommendations. She reminded Gloss who was in charge. There were ten U.S. magazines where the photos were also dropping over the next week.

I'm sure I'll hear from Bleek soon. Marie thought.

CHAPTER NINE

Bleek and Anastasia never left the beach house. Sunday was a rainy day and they spent it making love, exploring each other and conversing on the balcony. Neither wanted to leave but they had to. They left at ten pm, arriving at Anastasia's after midnight. They both wanted him to stay but knew it was best if he didn't. They kissed at her door.

"Good morning Anastasia."

"Good morning Bleek."

Bleek looked at his phone once he was in his truck. There were missed calls from Frederick, Robert, Gloss and Marie.

I'll call them later. They're not intruding on how I'm feeling.

¥¥¥¥¥

Bleek arrived in the conference room at seven-forty five. The only person in the room was Anastasia. She glanced up from her computer and gave him a smile. She was in the chair next to his, the chair she chose day one. He sat next to her, allowing his knee to brush hers under the table.

"Bleek." She said. He grinned and picked up a bottle of water.

The others filtered in, including Marie and a stormy-faced Gloss. Bleek looked to Frederick who shrugged. Marie walked to the front of the room which made Bleek sit up straighter. *Something is amiss.* He still hadn't checked his phone.

"Good morning. I'm here because our new ad campaign has hit the magazine and newsstands. I'm very pleased with it. Gloss, please turn on the video or whatever it's called." Marie said, pointing to a whiteboard.

The lights lowered as a screen dropped. Within seconds the cover from *International Horse Magazine* appeared on the screen. Anastasia stared unable to look away. Bleek's eyes moved around the room and saw no one was surprised but him and Anastasia. He started laughing from deep in his belly. Everyone looked at him with differing degrees of shock. That wasn't the response they expected. He stood and made his way to the front of the room.

"I must say timing is everything. When we took these photos weeks ago, I impulsively asked Anastasia to join me. The timing part comes in because Anastasia Wright is officially my woman and these couldn't be more appropriate."

Audible gasps were heard around the room. Even Frederick who was usually in the know was surprised. All eyes went to Anastasia who waved and smiled. Marie started clapping.

"Won't he do it." Marie said, hugging her son. Gloss scraped her chair back and stormed from the room.

"This changes nothing with Ms. Wright's role as lead attorney. Anastasia?" Bleek said.

"What Bleek said." She said and the managers, including Nathaniel stood and applauded. Marie walked over to Anastasia and opened her arms. Anastasia stood and embraced her, her face flaming hot.

"Now, let's get to the business of the week." Bleek said, returning to his seat. Marie kissed his forehead and left the room.

¥¥¥¥¥

After the meeting Anastasia left with the other managers. She needed to process the past two hours. *He claimed me in front of everyone. As his woman. I know what happened this weekend but just claiming?*

Gloss strutted into the room where Bleek still was within minutes.

"Was this your plan from the beginning?" She asked.

"Gloss, my plans are not your business." Bleek said mildly but his glance was steely.

"PR doesn't even seem to be my business either. Your mother made decisions on all of the photos."

"As is her right and in your contract."

"I won't work like this!"

"That's your choice Gloss. If you decide to resign, you will be compensated for the months remaining on your contract plus severance. You served Blackmon Ranch well."

"Fuck you Bleek. Fuck you." She exclaimed, stomping from the room.

"I'll have Robert draw you a check."

Gloss was infuriated but by the time she was outside but she was only furious with herself. She had just thrown away the best job she ever had over dick she hadn't had in years. She was on her way to Anastasia's office when Marie and Robert stepped in her path.

"Don't do it Gloss, trust me, it won't be worth it." Marie said kindly. Gloss didn't respond but followed Robert, her head held high.

¥¥¥¥¥

Bleek waited fifteen minutes in the canteen for Anastasia to arrive. He hadn't spoken to her since the meeting. He signed off on Gloss' six figure severance package and gone into a second meeting with Fredrick and Nathaniel that lasted until lunchtime. He stepped into the kitchen where Juan was.

"She eat in office today." Juan said before Bleek could ask. Turning on his heel, Bleek made his way across the property to Anastasia's. Her door was closed but he opened it and walked in. She was standing at her window, the lunch from Juan on the table unopened. Bleek walked up behind her.

"You're okay?" He asked.

"Of course, I'm just processing how to recover from me finding out I'm your woman at the same time as everyone else."

She didn't turn around. Rather than touch her, Bleek stepped in front of her.

"Anastasia, after this weekend, who else's woman would you be?" He asked softly but there was something hard in his tone. "I took you where no one other than my father and the cleaning person has ever been. I exposed my heart and soul to you and you to me. *You* allowed me inside you unsheathed several times, no questions asked. That makes you, at least in my mind, my woman. I know you well enough to know that's not how you operate. Do I wish we had been able to do it differently, perhaps tell our parents and then everyone else but life intervened. You're my woman Anastasia."

She allowed herself to look into his eyes and see that behind his strong words was vulnerability. Everything he said was accurate.

"Bleek, put like that, I'm your woman. But that was a lot."

He drew her into his arms, enfolding her close to his rapidly beating heart.

"It was but not nearly as much as there would have been if you had denied me."

A smile played around her lips.

"What, were you going to throw me over your shoulder and take me to your lair?"

"Whatever it took. You do need to see my lair but first let's walk to lunch and eat as we have since day one. Besides, Juan was frying garlic chicken when I left. Since, I don't smell garlic in here, it's safe to say you don't have any."

"Fried as in lard?"

"Yes ma'am. Let's go."

"If you insist."

"I do." He kissed her lightly before following her out.

This woman, my woman. He thought trying not to look at her perfect ass, and failing.

When they walked in Nathaniel glanced at Frederick.

"He's a G. I ain't mad at all. He deserves her —almost." Nathaniel said.

"I hear you my brother, I do. Some women makes a brother want to be a G."

"I know, I didn't want to be a player no more when I'm around her. Not that I ever had a shot." Nathaniel said almost wistfully. Frederick glanced at him but his sly smile was evident.

The canteen was full and everyone was surreptitiously watching Bleek. His eyes were all over Anastasia, a big grin on his usually stoic face.

"Hello." Anastasia and Bleek turned towards the voice. As soon as Bleek saw him, he knew it was Joel Wright. He quickly stood.

"Hello sir, I'm Bleek Blackmon." Anastasia looked on, chewing thoughtfully. Joel *never* showed up. And—he was dressed in his principal clothing. A blue suit with a lighter blue shirt with a pink and blue tie.

"I know who you are young man. I just want to know when was I going to know who was squiring my daughter around, since it's now international news."

Bleek stood almost at attention, respectful of Joel's position. His guys were all alert.

"Sir, I asked Anastasia if I could squire, I mean take her for a drive and she agreed. I can't apologize for that. I do apologize for it becoming international news before you knew. Mr. Wright, I care for and respect your daughter fully and will do my best by her." The men were of equal height at six feet and four inches and stood eye to eye. Joel finally offered Bleek his hand and Bleek shook it firmly.

"That's all a father can ask. Anastasia?"

"Hey dad. You look nice, all suited up. This chicken is so good, you should have some since you drove forty miles and all." Bleek looked from Anastasia to Joel who was grinning at his daughter. *She talks trash to everyone.*

Joel glanced at Bleek and shrugged which made Bleek chuckle. Anastasia stood and hugged her dad. Everyone was openly staring by this point. Anastasia said to the room, "This is my dad everyone. He's retired principal Joel Wright and came to make sure, my *man* treats this woman the Wright way. Otherwise a duel might have ensued."

Laughter filled the room, Bleek's the loudest. Juan walked out with a plate filled with fried chicken, sweet potatoes and roasted Brussels sprouts. Joel took a seat, declaring, "I might as well."

"So, dad where's your woman?"

"She told me I could come up here and make a fool of myself but she wasn't watching. I almost left after all the questions and cavity searches at the gate. I was like man, we aren't close like that." Joel said. Bleek looked stricken for a second until he realized Joel was kidding about the searches. "A man name Robert finally came out and took a DNA test and escorted me here in shackles."

Bleek almost choked laughing. The man was standup comedy funny and dry with it.

"Now you can see where my sense of humor comes from. I get this ugly face, these long legs and sarcasm from *him.*

"You're ugly, I'm not." Joel said. Bleek was close to sliding out of his chair from relief and the way they communicated.

Joel and Bleek talked horses and fishing. Anastasia ate her food and relaxed into her current reality. She had a man, whose mom was cool and more importantly who was cool with her dad. Not being cool with her dad wasn't a total dealbreaker but it would be a deficit. Joel, was the coolest person and parent, he gave the benefit of the doubt and left it up to those he encountered to change it. Sage, on the other hand, you had to prove yourself to.

"I have a job, I'm leaving you to it. Dad, behave." Anastasia said as she waved and left the canteen. All eyes were on her, especially Bleek's.

"Bleek, her heart is huge and she's brilliant, confident and mouthy and I still feel you got the best deal. That's my baby, I'm entrusting to you." Joel said seriously.

"Sir, I'm honored and I've seen and experienced the brilliance and other attributes, I'll say this, I'm not worthy but I'm in it to win it."

Joel held up his fist, Bleek pounded it.

"My man." Joel said. "I will need some of that chicken to go. Sage is on some kind of health kick and fried chicken isn't on it."

"I got you. We have care packages." Bleek said. Juan handed him a package before he could ask. *The man hears everything.*

"Thanks Sir." Bleek said to Juan. He walked Joel to his car. Uninvited guests had to leave their cars at the gate and get driven inside. The security was intense.

"We will have a meal soon." Joel said. "Your mother included."

"Sir, I'm sure Marie Blackmon is already planning something. She's #TeamAnastasia." Bleek offered his hand but Joel pulled him into an embrace.

What a crazy day. Bleek thought but he had an added pep to his step. The radio on his hip buzzed.

"Hello."

"We have a few foals in trouble." Nathaniel said, the stress evident in his voice. "I'm down here with Frederick and I don't know shit about horses. West stables."

"I'm on my way." Jake did a u-turn and headed west. "It's all in a day at Blackmon Ranch."

Six hours later he phoned Anastasia.

"Hello, I'm sorry I wasn't there at five. I had to deliver baby horses. Frederick's staff wasn't prepared because they weren't due yet and Nathaniel made it clear he's about cattle not M'fing horses."

"No sorry, that's your job. I'm on the way home."

"Okay, I was planning to bring you home with me but I'm covered in blood, horseshit and mud and everything hurts. I'll call you?"

"I'll answer but you can just gallop over to my house, I have a huge tub you can soak in and

I'll scrub your back and feed you leftover fried chicken but if you would rather…"

"Don't try to back out now. I'll take off these clothes and trash them but I'm on my way."

She's going to feed me, wash my back—and I might even get to eat her desserts—that's where my love struck ass is going."

"I haven't been in a tub since I was a shorty." Bleek said, sitting in the tub with Anastasia an hour later. He showered and changed after calling her but accepted the tub—with her.

"You've been missing out. It seems men become tub averse or something. Mom and dad have been in their home twenty years and dad has never graced the tub."

"I guess we don't think it's manly, especially all oily and soapy. Men have reps to maintain."

"Who y'all telling you took a tub bath… nobody. That's just nuts. Your woman loves a tub full of oils, soap—and now my man."

The words my man made Bleek lick his lip.

"I like your tongue…" Anastasia murmured. "It's long, strong and talented.

"It's all yours…" Bleek said, sticking it out.

CHAPTER TEN

A couple of weeks after Gloss left a blind item appeared in Central Florida's Black News You Can Use gossip weekly.

Mail Order Attorney or is it Bride?

It seems the reclusive almost nomadic rancher and the Blackest wealthy cow-man we know, Bleek Blackmon, even his name is fine; Not that we know him but we are getting glimpses. Just this week he appeared in some ads for his complex, I mean ranch and honey his main attorney, owner of The Wright Way Law Firm, Lady Anastasia stole the show from him and the horses. Honey is gorgeous and looks built to ride…but anyway it seems there are those who thinks she might have been negotiated for. I mean she's only been his attorney for a couple months but her contract is significant, like a couple millions per year but I don't know but maybe that's the cost these days to be with a boss—and clearly Anastasia Wright is a boss, the Wright way honeys and either no one's mad or everybody is. Until we know more, hee haw!

"I'm going to…" Bleek started but Anastasia leaned across the counter, touching him.

"Do nothing. As your lead attorney and as the mail order attorney Lady Anastasia my advice professional and personal is to ignore it. Blackmon Ranch will not stoop to such low places." She said, speaking in what Bleek named her lawyer voice. He leaned back a bit, her being that close was a constant distraction.

They were meeting their parents for dinner. They had dined with Maria and The Wrights separately but this was their night for all five to dine together in a neutral environment. Maria was coming with Raymond Liles, a family 'friend' he suspected she was quietly dating. Raymond was seventy-five and lost his wife a year before Bleek Jr. passed. The couples had been close friends, Raymond was a retired equine veterinarian who worked closely with Bleek Jr. for years.

"I'll trust the personal on this one. But it better stop or I'll do things the Bleek Blackmon way."

"I'm intrigued to know about this Bleek Blackmon way, the ways I've seen to this point, after the first impressions of course have been excellent."

"I see you keep me grounded by reminding me of first impressions—but there's a few men in here, a couple it's best not to unleash."

Anastasia pretended to shudder.

"I'm even more intrigued but we have to make impressions."

¥¥¥¥¥

Bleek and Anastasia arrived after Maria and Raymond. The huge vintage Lincoln Continental parked up front was the tell. There was only one in the state and it was owned by Raymond, a gift from Bleek Jr. It was in mint condition.

"That's Raymond's car." Bleek said.

"That's a beauty. I bet he drives it slow."

"You know it."

They were met at door by the hostess who led them to a private room in the old school steakhouse. Bleek's parents loved it but Bleek tolerated it. It was one of those places Black and native Americans could only work until they were forced to open to everyone. The food was admittedly good.
Joel and Sage were led in behind them. Anastasia smiled, at seventy her mama was beautiful and shapely wearing a red dress at the knee with white piping at the neckline and sleeves. Her heels were three inches tall.

Sage did two hours of yoga and stretch daily. Anastasia noticed Marie openly assessing her, likely trying to guess her age. She easily looked late fifties. Maria on the other hand was an elegantly pretty woman who looked her age mostly due to her attire, heavy jewels and makeup. She was trim from horse riding. After the air kisses were done, Marie announced she ordered for everyone.

"How is that possible?" Sage asked. "How would you know what everyone wanted?" Anastasia sat back a bit. She couldn't wait to see how this played out. Sage did *not* eat beef or pork.
"It's a steakhouse so I was sure everyone wanted steak and of course creamed spinach and baked potatoes." Maria said.

"I'm going to have to ask for roasted chicken and sautéed spinach. I don't eat red meat or foods heavy in sugar or butter."

"There's no fun in that but suit yourself." Maria pulled out her phone and *phoned* the kitchen. "Is dry aged ribeye medium good for everyone else?" Everyone else nodded except Bleek.

"I think I'll have the steak and roasted chicken please." Maria shot him a look, he ignored.

"I'll take that as well." Raymond said. He hadn't stopped ogling Sage since they walked in. Maria's lips became a thin line but she amended the order.

"If I were braver, I might have as well but I'm used to being ordered around by women. I just eat what's on my plate." Joel said drily. Bleek couldn't hold back his laughter. Joel was his kind of cool. Both older women had pressed lips. Anastasia was buttering and eating bits of bread. "Raymond what's your role at the ranch?"

"He's my friend." Marie interjected.

"I'm their retired horse veterinarian. Marie and I are lifelong friends. What do you do?" Raymond asked.

"Not a lot. I'm a retired principal for the past ten years and do enough not to make a ruckus. I'm married to a beautiful woman for forty years, I have a brilliant daughter and I owe no one. Life is great." Bleek could hardly contain himself. He couldn't recall being so entertained. Anastasia was still buttering bread.

"You do love bread, Anastasia." Marie said.

"I do and real butter. I'm a yoga and stretch enthusiast like my mom, I'm also riding daily. I'm just not one to deprive myself of food I love. Some days I eat a basket of bread, other days half a cake, I barely drink alcohol though." Anastasia shrugged like it was all just above her head. Everyone except Anastasia had bourbon. She handled Marie and Sage in one short phrase. Bleek reached over and hugged her. The waiters brought out the food, thankfully.

Dinner was an hour of discussing varied things going on in the surrounding areas and the world. At the one hour mark after the meal was served, Maria announced her departure.

"I must head to the ranch. Tonight has been delightful, just delightful." She said. The men stood as she hugged Bleek and Anastasia. She waved her fingers at Sage.

"We are leaving as well." Joel said. "Pray for me Bleek, it's a long ride to Gainesville and I'm sure I'm either in the outhouse or the doghouse, only Sage knows for sure." Bleek held back more laughter.

"If he continues to run his mouth he's going to be at Anastasia's house." Sage said. Joel took her hand and held it aloft. Bleek had to look away. The man was hilarious. Bleek hugged Sage and Joel. Anastasia blew kisses.

"Your dad is funny. He could do standup." Bleek said.

"He is. My mom's sense of humor is different."

"My mom has one but on her own terms. I'm sure she's going on to Raymond about him drooling over your mom. How old is your mom ?"

"She's seventy. I promise you I won't be that fit at seventy but I'll be juicy. Not that I'm indicating you will see me at seventy by any means."

Don't say a word Bleek. Bleek could almost hear Joel saying that in his ear. He picked up the leather payment folder and added his card.

"My mom always orders the most expensive items and never pays, though it's her invite." Bleek said.

"When I'm older I plan to do the same. There's got to be perks."

"I got perks for you." Bleek said, eyeing her hungrily. His mouth on her and him inside her had become his weakness. Her desire and ferocity for him matched his for her. They couldn't get enough of each other.

"Your place is closer and I do need to work off that bread and butter."

"I'm going to butter your buns Anastasia."

"Oh, you're so nasty...I do like your nasty."

"Waiter!" Bleek yelled.

¥¥¥¥¥

"Joel, you're too much. You know no one should order for anyone." Sage said. They were taking U.S. 441 home. It wasn't the busier interstate and a longer more leisurely drive home.

"I am too much but I don't know what anyone should do. I would have simply said, "I would like to order roast chicken instead of asking how she could do that. It's clearly something she could and has done repeatedly. The woman phoned the chef." Sage sucked her teeth. That's exactly what Joel would have done.

"I'm not you Joel. Marie is pushy."

"I'm sure that's true. The thing is she likes Anastasia and Anastasia likes her, I'm on the side of them continuing on that path not ruined by her parents. When she commented on her bread eating, Anastasia checked her so kindly it felt like art but I assure you she will not comment in that way again. But Sage, I love your combat prepared nature."

"Whatever, Joel. Everyone isn't the life of the party."

"That's nothing but facts and then there's me. Wait until I spin her around the dance floor, I'll be her new best friend who wasn't friends with her husband."

Sage tried not to laugh but Joel was Joel.

"You're a nut."

"I hope this is the night you crave nuts." Sage poked out her lips at him. The loving wasn't as regular but just as good.

¥¥¥¥¥

"Sage is wound a little tight but is attractive enough. She dresses too young. You could almost see the muscles in her belly." Marie said.

"Could you?" Raymond asked rhetorically.

Marie loved venting and he was who she chose to vent to. He had been in love with her before she met Bleek Jr. and never stopped throughout their marriages. He was her confidante even during her marriage though they never crossed any sexual lines. His wife tolerated it and if Bleek Jr. noticed it, he was too confident to care. Bleek Jr. knew Marie was all his from the day he laid eyes on her at a ball. It took him years to marry her but she was his from that point on. Marie continued talking, Raymond nodded or responded as appropriate.

¥¥¥¥¥

Buried deep inside Anastasia Bleek felt he was finally home. He couldn't have articulated if he tried. It was beyond sex, that was for sure. He had enjoyed sex since age sixteen and he didn't engage except to give and receive pleasure. He recalled Bleek Jr. talking to him when he asked for condoms.

Son, sex is more than sexual organs grinding together. Don't touch a woman you don't plan to please. Otherwise take care of that in the shower. Mind you great sex will not make you fall in love but women will fall in love with you because unfortunately too many men are in it for their pleasure and leave a woman lacking. Sadly, too many women will never say the sex isn't good—to you. But you will know. Take your time.

He knew the first time he touched Anastasia, kissed her, that this wasn't sex, he was finally making love.

"Anastasia."

"Mmm." She murmured, her eyes glazed over slits of pleasure.

"I love you."

"I love you."

Her love walls caressed him, drawing him in deep—deeper.

She loves ME.

CHAPTER ELEVEN

IT SEEMS SHE'S ALWAYS BEEN ABOUT THE PAID ONES

Lady Anastasia has been involved with the money boys from day one. Fourteen years ago she was seen dancing with the one and only Eli Abrams, one of Manhattan's most noted attorneys. There was a photo of a younger Anastasia dancing close to the son of Eli Abrams Sr. a world famous Jewish attorney and Audra Abrams, famed African American opera singer. *And a mere three years ago, she's seen dancing cheek to cheek with none other than Ashad Williams, the young baller from down south, one of her most paid— clients. Mind you, her current beau, Black cowboy with a quietly held PHD in equestrian biology but cowboys don't flaunt their intellect has mo money than both with land to boot...so he might be the one.* There was a photo of Anastasia and Ashad holding up the championship trophy his team won that year with his arms draped around her, huge smiles on both faces. The third photo was of her and Bleek on their horses.

Bleek read the article three times, rage filling his blood. This was vintage Gloss and she was going to pay. But what disturbed him was Anastasia with Abrams and Williams. He knew she had dated but something he never felt before enveloped him. He was *jealous.* He had never cared what a woman did but seeing *his* Anastasia in photos, old photos before he knew she existed filled his gut with bile green jealousy.

"Bleek, that woman is thirty-six, of course she's dated." Frederick said. Bleek looked up remembering Fredrick was in the room.

"Fredrick, that woman is going—to be my wife and I know that. I'm for damn sure in no position to be—whatever I am but damn it I am."

"You am jealous." Frederick said. "It must be love then."

Bleek shot Frederick a glance but Frederick chuckled. One of Frederick's roles in Bleek's life was to be honest.

"Man, I want to, hell yea I'm jealous. I'm going to ruin Gloss' life. She went too far with this. Come for me but coming for her, twice. Nah."

"I feel you my brother. But have you spoken to Anastasia because a couple of weeks ago she said let sleeping dogs sleep."

"I did not. This is all Bleek. I told Robert to send someone to retrieve all of Blackmon property. Her home office was bought and paid for by the ranch, the computers, cameras, podcast shit, all of it. It's mine and she won't do this with that." Frederick grinned in approval. Bleek was hard to press but when pressed you paid lessons. "The community college should be there right about now, picking up everything, even the furniture. Robert said it's over a hundred grand in shit—I own. If she doesn't cool her heels, her contracts will dry up." Bleek said, his voice low and hard. "If I'm good to you, you better know what you're doing when you come for me and mine. By the way I sent a couple of reporters. Let's get this work done, I need to talk to my woman." Frederick got up and followed Bleek to the horses, a couple of the recent foals needed special care.

¥¥¥¥¥

Gloss raged and cussed at the top of her lungs when the college arrived with orders to retrieve her entire office. She tried blocking them but the plainclothes police officer told her to comply or get arrested. She tried calling Bleek several times but the calls went straight to voice mail. She was advised by several people to not cross Bleek but her jealousy and desire to hurt him and Anastasia fueled her. When everything was done, a woman walked up to her, "I recorded everything that happened here today. I'll give the recording to Mr. Blackmon and what he does with it, will depend entirely on what you do going forward."

Gloss dropped to the floor in her now mostly empty office. There were personal belongings scattered in neat piles but everything was gone. She wept finally. After weeping she phoned Marie.

"How could he do this? I was good to Blackmon Ranch."

Marie listened, no sympathy in her heart. Gloss went too far.

"Gloss, you went to far, first by threatening to quit, secondly by cussing Bleek who fed you and mostly by going after a woman he loves. You bought this. It would behoove you to move on quietly."

"But to take my equipment." Gloss said. "That was petty and mean."

"This started with your petty meanness and ended with his. Let it go. You were paid top dollar for years and was given the equivalent of two years salary—let it go."

Gloss didn't like the answer but she heard loud and clear what Marie was and wasn't saying. If she did anything else it would be more than Bleek coming for her. She softly thanked Marie and hung up.

It's time to get away from this hell-hole. She muttered but knew she would likely never have as good a situation.

¥¥¥¥¥

Anastasia received calls from her parents, Eli, and Ashad asking if she were okay. She assured them all she was but she was furious. She clerked for Eli the summer after her first year of law school and the picture was of them celebrating a win she assisted in. In the photo she was twenty-two and Eli thirty-nine. The photo was taken by Sara, Eli's fiancé at the time. The photo of her and Ashad was taken after he thanked her publicly after winning his first championship. She was thirty-three then to his twenty three and he always flirted with her but it was nothing more than fun. She didn't appreciate being portrayed as something she wasn't. A knock on her door made her refocus. It was Robert. He had become her friend. He told her what occurred with Gloss.

"Robert, that's her bed. She chose it." Anastasia said. Bleek told her the next time Gloss did something he would handle it and he had. Her phone rang, it was Sage.

"Turn on your television, local news." Sage said. Anastasia picked up the remote and turned on to the television. There was a reporter talking to Eli and his wife and Ashad via teleconference.

"I don't usually respond to rumors or slander." Eli said. "But in this case I'm going to address it. Anastasia Wright clerked for me her first summer after law school. The photo you saw in that trashy column was of us celebrating a case she worked on with me and which her research won. If you decide to come for family, my family and she's family then be prepared. Anastasia we love you and our daughters, your goddaughters, love you as well." Eli said. His wife chimed in with her love.

"Like the lawyer, I consider Anastasia family too. I have to admit I was a young knucklehead and tried to get my flirt on." Ashad said but she shut my young a—I mean self down." Anastasia smiled, she often told him to clean up his language. "Anastasia is big sis all day and she's clearly got people. Not that she needs them but we out here. Anastasia like you told me, don't be bothered by tricks, or something like that." Giggles flew from Anastasia and her anger dissolved.

"You heard it here first." The reporter said before the story changed. Anastasia turned off the television.

"Robert?"

He grinned at her as he stood, "like the young brother says, you have people."

"He said, "I *got* people."

"What he said."

It's nice to have people. But if Ms. Gloss doesn't slow her roll, I'm going to see her. Anastasia mused before getting back to work.

¥¥¥¥¥

Bleek walked into Frederick's office after washing the muck off him and changing. The foals were doing well but two of them would become ranch horses. Coming early had done something to stunt their growth but Blackmon nurtured those as much as the ones who brought in great fees and sales. Bleek was hands on with his horses. He was glad to see food on the table. They worked through lunch. After he was seated Frederick turned on the television and replayed the interview. Bleek watched while he ate.

"I guess it's good I didn't take my jealous ass to talk to Anastasia earlier, eh." He said.

"It's a great thing Bleek Blackmon." Anastasia said walking into the office. Frederick prepared to leave but she gave him a look and he returned to his seat. Bleek chewed thoughtfully, watching her. Her face was inscrutable and she was wearing a black dress, hitting mid-thigh with black stilettos, her hair slicked back in a twist and her lips red. "It's a great thing because if you had brought said ass to my office and said something crazy because your former— whatever she was to you, tried to scandalize my name, you my love would have been handed said ass. In the future—please let this woman, your woman and attorney, know what tactics you are taking because if that same ass—ends up in court, she as in I, is who will stand beside you. Of course Robert reinforced it was your property to take. However, in the future, let's retrieve Blackmon Ranch property at the time of dismissal not after you're pissed off. I'm glad my *friends* eased your jealousy. Enjoy your meal, I will see you at my house once you're done here." She turned on her heel and walked from the room but stopped at the door, looking over her shoulder. "Give me a couple of hours before you follow me. It's best for both of us."

Bleek was glad he was sitting behind the table because he was so turned on he felt lightheaded. She had handed him his ass— and properly and with a witness.

"I am so shook for you my brother." Fredrick said. "In fact I'm just shook. Sir, that woman, your woman, kicked your ass without raising a foot or her voice."

"You're shook? I'm scared to go over there and I'm scared not to."

"I would err on the side of going, but that's just me. Man..."

"I'm so glad she's team Blackmon."

"Nigga, that woman is team Bleek."

"Yea." Bleek said, cockily. "Hell yea."

¥¥¥¥¥

Two hours later, Anastasia opened the door allowing Bleek inside. She was wearing old, baggy sweats and her hair was free. He pulled her into an embrace.

"Are we good?" He asked, looking into her eyes.

"We are. We need to talk though."

He followed her through the house to the sunroom at the back of her home. It was like a living room-library with windows as walls.

Her yard looked like a forest. She sat on the loveseat and he joined her.

"Bleek, what was Gloss to you?"

"Gloss was hired to do PR. My mom hired her. She felt we needed a public presence and she came highly recommended. We worked together and I found her cool. We had sex several times over the course of a couple of years. A situation of mutuality but men seem to often get that wrong. A couple of years ago I ended it, knowing it was just what it was and wasn't going to lead her on further. Since then she's done her job and tried flirting a few times but I rebuffed that and allowed her to work mostly with mom and Robert. Anastasia, I treat my people well but you will not bite my hand after I fed you and *no one* will disrespect you." He said, his voice resolute. "And yes I was jealous seeing you in those photos not because I had any idea if you dated them or not but because I'm human and I love you. I never gave a damn who a woman slept with or dated before or after me. But you're not a woman, you're now my woman."

"Bleek, I have a past, there were men I dated and was sexual with." He winced at the sexual reference.

"I know that. I'm just telling you how I reacted. How I felt."

"That's fair. All of it's fair but it's exhausting. I will beat Gloss' ass though." Bleek's mouth opened and closed.

"As in a fight?"

"Nope, as in smacking her in the head and dragging her by the expensive weave across this ranch and back."

"You do have thug tendencies. Who knew?"

"Anyone who ever tried me and thought I couldn't handle myself. Joel taught me to box and Sage to never let any one disrespect me but once. Gloss got two."

"Box as in Muhammad Ali boxing?"

"No as in Billy Blanks. Sage had me meditating and stretching, Joel kick boxing, horse riding and trash talking. Bleek, I've had to take care of me for a good while now. I love your protectiveness but I promise you the next time she bucks I'm knucking, that's it."

"I don't know if I'm scared or what. Your friends were ready to buck and knuck."

"Because they know, I don't mess with anyone and I've dug my own gold. Mind you I'm not ashamed to admit if you didn't work at something you were not going to get far with me. Mind you I said *were.* Bleek, I'm all manned up." He grinned lazily.

"Yes you are because if you had been on some dismissing me because I'm a mere man thing, I was kidnapping you. Straight up."

"Where would we go?" She asked. He peered at her curiously.

"Where would you like to go?"

"With you, anywhere."

"I'm going to Brazil for four days next week, you want to fly?"

"Only if my boss approves."

"I could probably convince him. Your team is solid. Anastasia…"

"Yes."

"I'm tired as hell. Can I sleep?"

"Only if I can sleep with you." She grabbed his hand and led him to her bed. They slept.

¥¥¥¥¥

Rio was everything Anastasia heard and more. Bleek worked days and she worked in the hotel room but at night they saw all the sites and danced in the streets. He took off the day before they left and they went to the rain forest. That was her favorite experience of the trip. The most surprising was Bleek speaking Portuguese with no American inflection. Getting to know him was thrilling. She asked him about why he never mentioned having a PHD.

"I do nothing to try to impress people. If they wish to think I'm an uncultured cowboy, I'm cool with that. My dad always led with it when introducing me. My mom insisted on me getting educated. I was in college from sixteen to twenty four getting three degrees and worked the ranch as well. I love knowing things for knowing's sake not to impress white folks or our folks. Bleek Blackmon needs no accolades. I'm good."

"Well, I'm impressed even more so because of how humble you are—well not humble exactly because you can be arrogant but you know what I mean. This has been my best trip. I've been to Canada, several European countries and all over the Caribbean but this. Morocco and Greece are on my bucket list."

"We can make that happen. I'm glad you're here. Usually, it's me and Frederick doing business and drinking way too much Brazilian rum. This is—I've never traveled with a woman, I'm a virgin."

"I'm so glad to get that cherry then. Bleek, you are an anomaly and I'm..."

"I know baby, me too. This is the best trip. I love you."

"Let's get in that bed, so you can show me what that love feels like. I need that kind where you have your way with me, pushing me beyond my limits, tattooing my insides with your love."

"I am in heaven. I don't know what I did to get you but I pray I keep doing it. Damn woman."

"I love it when you call me woman." Bleek picked her up and carried her to the bed. He had never felt more like a man in his life.

CHAPTER TWELVE

The first meeting after Brazil, Robert announced Gloss moved to Atlanta and was working in the music industry. Anastasia didn't respond. Gloss was a non-factor for her. Bleek wasn't in the meeting. The annual rodeo was coming on Friday and that was his focus. In fact only Anastasia, Robert, Marie and Sylvester Beeman, the new PR person was there. They were getting Sylvester ready to go because the rodeo was a huge PR event. Cowboys came from all over to participate.

"I need to get to my office." Anastasia said. "Welcome Sylvester. Mrs. Blackmon is your main contact, Robert pays for everything and I'm legal." He stood shaking her hand. Sylvester was a proud gay man who was confident and not intimidated by working around cowboys. Being six feet, six inches was likely conducive to that.

Anastasia was fielding calls and e-mails when Robert stepped into her office—she tried to mask annoyance because he knew how busy they all were. There was a stricken look on his face. Before she could inquire, a young man walked in and her mouth flew open. He appeared to be about nineteen but except for his light brown complexion he looked as if Bleek gave birth to him. The height, size and the proud way he held his head. He looked overwhelmed.

Bleek has a son. She thought.

"Anastasia, this young man says he's Bleek's nephew." Robert said.

"Nephew?" Anastasia asked. Robert nodded, he knew where her thoughts had gone. The boy looked cloned.

"I can speak." The young man said. "My dad died several weeks ago. My grandmother said Bleek Blackmon Jr. was my grandad. My mom passed when I was a kid and my grandma and dad raised me." Anastasia's heart surged for the young man and she suddenly felt tired.

"What's your name and please have a seat?" Anastasia said. "I'm Anastasia Wright, the..."

"I know who you are. I saw you in the magazines. That's how my grandma found him. My name is Blade like my daddy. My granddad gave them money to keep quiet. Grandma gave me the last five grand to come here, she was twenty one when she had my dad, he was forty-three. The checks stopped coming about a year ago." Blade said. He was trying to appear tough but he was clearly nervous. *The money dried up when Bleek Jr. died.* Anastasia glanced at Robert and in that moment she knew he was aware.

"Are you in school?"

"I graduated high school last year. My dad was only thirty eight, he had sickle cell disease. I don't have it. I work as a casual at the post office in New Orleans, that's where I'm from." He said. Anastasia knew a casual was hired without benefits and for a week less than a year. They often got rehired but wasn't guaranteed.

"Are you hungry?" She asked.

"I could eat." He said.

"Robert, please get some food for Blade. No one is to know until Bleek knows."

"Of course." Robert looked relieved to leave.

"What's he like? This place looks like Busch Gardens or something." Blade asked, looking around.

"Bleek is the best man I've ever met yet he's tough. This is going to shock him."

"I guess he didn't know his dad had another kid. My dad didn't talk about him. No one did until dad died and they showed me the papers and magazines. I kind of favor him."

"Yes, you do. Did you drive here?"

"No ma'am. My hoopty is for local driving, I flew to Orlando and got a cab here."

Robert walked in with two plates of food fifteen minutes later. Blade looked exhausted and more than a little intimidated.

"There's a bathroom in there. I'll be right back." Anastasia said. She pointed to the hall and Robert followed her. "Who besides you knows about this and don't deny you knew that there was a son?"

"No one but Ms. Blackmon likely knows. Bleek Jr. was a rolling stone. It's a miracle there aren't others but he had surgery after Blade was born. I didn't know there was a grandson."

Horror filled Anastasia at his words. That's why after the one son, or rather the one not born to Marie, he had gotten a vasectomy.

"This is terrible and no fault of that kid. Wherever Bleek is get him here." She demanded and walked inside. Blade was devouring a plate of ribs. There was another plate with burgers, fries and fruit.

It took forty-five minutes for Bleek to get there. His eyes lit on Anastasia filled with concern, she pointed to Blade. The look and reaction from Bleek would have been comical if it weren't so bad. He looked, squinted, looked again and back at Anastasia. Blade had a mock hard look on his face, his chin up defiantly as Bleek assessed him. It was the mask of many black teens in situations they couldn't control.

"Who in the hell is this?" Bleek asked. Blade stood and walked up to Bleek. He stopped inches from him. Their profiles were uncannily similar.

"I'm Blade, your half-brother's son." As if in slow motion Bleek looked from him to Anastasia and back before dropping in the closest chair. Anastasia walked over and sat on the arm, relaying Blade's story. Bleek stared at the young man as Anastasia spoke unable to look away. It was as if someone took his face and body, slimmed it by fifty pounds and gave it lighter skin and said, "Here is your clone."

"Blade — I'm sorry about your parents and about my dad, I had no idea you or your father existed. Who else other than your grandmother knows?" Blade shrugged and sat down, he looked tired and lost.

"I don't know. I'm not looking for anything I just needed to know." He said, his voice trembling.

"Sure you do. If you're my nephew and everything looks like you are, this is your home." Bleek finally got up and stood in front of Blade. "Stand up." Blade stood and Bleek embraced him. "Man, this isn't on you, this is on my dad, your grandfather. Do you have any things?"

Bleek looked around for bags.

"That older man has them. I caught a taxi here from the airport. I can go to a hotel."

"The hell you will. You're coming home with me. I'm going to have to get us tested. We have a doctor on staff who can take our blood." Blade nodded and pulled out a phone. He found a picture of his father and handed the phone to Bleek.

"I'll be damned, your dad looks more like me than I do. I had a little brother. This is some bullshit. Bullshit!" Bleek finally wanted to hit something but Alexandra walked up and placed her hand on his back, calming him. He turned to face her, she saw the emotion and pain on his face. "Here I am living like a king and my brother is sick and dying. What kind of shit is that?" He sounded as lost as Blade looked.

"It's human shit Bleek. I'm going to get Dr. Stephens here and you need to decide how to break this to your mom. We cannot let the sun go down on this or hide Blade away. Blade what's your last name?"

"I'm Blade Black, the funny thing is grandma's last name is Black." Bleek laughed caustically, no humor in it. "My grandma is a good woman, she just felt it was time I knew my people. She told me he died."

"He did die Blade." Bleek said. He glanced at the clock and saw it was only two pm. It felt like days had passed since he walked in the room. He pulled out his phone and dialed Marie.

"Mom, are you still on the property?" Bleek asked. "Come to Anastasia's office, it's important." He said and hung up. Anastasia was on the phone making things happen. Bleek got up and sat beside Blade.

"Man, I'm sorry. I can't do anything about the past thirty-eight years but going forward I can. Did you live okay?"

"Yessir. My dad and my mom had sickle cell, they met at the doctors office as teens. According to grandma, her name is Bella, them both having it canceled mine out. He sent checks every month and we lived in a nice house. He bought that too. Dad was nineteen and mama seventeen when I was born. Mama died at twenty-three. We lived with grandma. I said that. I worked at the post office, I made twenty dollars an hour. I work hard and might get permanent." Bleek nodded listening. *There is no way in hell you're leaving here. If you're my blood...*

Dr. Stephen arrived first and asked Bleek and Blade to come with him. He took them into the bathroom for swabs and to draw blood.

"What's the emergency?" Marie asked walking into Anastasia's office.

"Bleek will explain." Anastasia said.

Bleek walked in with Blade followed by Dr. Fisher. The blood drained from Marie's face, her mouth opening and closing like a fish.

"I'm a grandma?"

"No ma'am, I guess the proper term would be you're a step-mama, this is Blade Black, your husband and my father's grandson." Bleek said. Marie screamed. She literally screamed. "No! No!" No one moved.

"I can't do this today. Bleek no, we can't do this." Marie said. Bleek moved close to his mom and placed both hands on her shoulders, facing her.

"Mom, today is all we have. Blade's father, Blade Sr. died at thirty-eight, less than a month ago. He never knew his dad or me and he's gone. If Blade is ours and I know he is, this is his home. You are beholden in no way but he's my blood, my nephew and he will be here with us."

Marie looked ten years older. Anastasia hurt for her, Bleek and Blade who were innocents in all of this.

"Bleek, please get Robert or someone to take me home. I need to go home." She hadn't looked at Blade since he walked in.

"Okay but Doc said we will have results as soon as he can process them. I'm announcing it tomorrow morning and the new PR person will do his thing. Mom, this isn't to hurt you but because wrongs need correcting. Did you know about Blade Sr?"

She nodded affirmatively but rushed out when she saw Robert.

"I'm going to the lab." Doctor Fisher said. Bleek turned to Blade who stood in the middle of the office.

"Welcome home Blade. Blackmon Ranch is your home. You will stay with me. Of course you know Anastasia is my—fiancé."

"Fiancé? I have not been proposed to, there's is no ring on this finger. Bleek Blackmon, you are going to have to stop assuming sh— things." Anastasia said full of attitude. Blade actually laughed. Bleek walked over to Anastasia and dropped to his knee, "Anastasia Wright, please, please, please be my fiancé. After I talk to your dad, your ring will bling. On God." Anastasia rolled her eyes but a huge smile was on her face. Blade looked on, wondering what kind of people these were.

"I'll say yes only until my dad agrees and I see the bling." She said. Bleek stood up and pulled her close.

"Thank you. I'm so glad for you because—I need you." He kissed her lightly.

"Blade, I know you must be tired. There's a bed in the room next to the bathroom." Anastasia said. "I have to take care of things —

"Yes ma'am. I am tired. I haven't slept much since—dad passed. He was a good dad."

"I'm sure he was." Bleek said. "Come with me." He led Blade to the small room that held a bed and chair. Roger often stayed over when there were pending legal issues.

"If you need anything reach out to Anastasia."

"Yessir, I'm not trying to be forward but Ms. Anastasia's, a real one." A genuine smile covered Bleek's face.

"The realest and she's my fiancé. But you were there. Get some rest." Bleek said before embracing the younger man and leaving the room.

Anastasia walked into his arms when he returned to the office.

"How are you?" She asked, sharing his pain.

"I don't even know. But I do know that's my nephew in there and no matter how he got here, *I'm* going to do right by him."

"You're a good man. Is your mom okay?"

"She will be. My dad wasn't an easy man to be married to. He was about this ranch first and foremost. Her pride is damaged more than anything. I don't think she cares there was a son but that the world will now know. She's an old school wife, sex ain't no biggie just don't let me see it."

"Well—Anastasia will not be that kind of wife. Trust and believe *that*."

"Oh, I do. I'm not my dad. I loved him Anastasia and he was a great father but—I'm not him. Do you own a piece?"

"I have a sig. Why?"

"Of course you do. It just popped in my head —I need to go and wrap up what I was working on, I'll be back in two hours, tops. Do you think Robert knew?"

"He did, he knew about Blake Sr. not Jr. Bleek, I need Robert, he's been more helpful to me than anyone." Bleek nodded. Robert was sixty-five and had worked for the ranch forty-four years. His loyalty at that time was to Bleek Jr. and the ranch in that order.

"His employment is safe. He was hired by and loyal to my father and as loyal to me and now you. He's family, firing him would be like firing mom. Now, if it were Fredrick who I hired, I would kick his ass but I couldn't fire him either—you are already making my life better.

A lot of craziness happens in this life." He kissed her and left the building.

Damn, I have a nephew, an heir and a fiancé. Go big Bleek. He said making his way to the horses. *God, I thank you for bringing Anastasia when you brought her. I know we don't talk as much as we should but thank you.* His phone buzzed and he sped up.

Marie phoned Anastasia an hour after Bleek left.

"Please talk some sense into Bleek. We will provide handsomely for the boy and his grandmother."

Anastasia felt deeply for her but she agreed with Bleek on everything regarding Blade. He was blood and that mattered. He had suffered enough.

"Bleek's mind is made up."

Marie hung up on her.

Bleek told Frederick what was going on.

"Man, you're a good one. Life can turn on a dime."

"True but as hard as it looks, it's the best my life has ever been. My woman is by my side on everything. Doing what I never knew I needed."

"That's your blessing my brother."

"Ayyyyyyye!"

¥¥¥¥¥

The next morning many national news stations and all Florida stations led with the story about Blade. Bleek stood with Blade and Anastasia at a conference the night before after the results proved Blade was indeed his blood and announced;

We discovered today that I have a nephew, Blade Black, soon to be Blade Black-Blackmon. He was born to my now deceased brother, Blade Black Sr. and his girlfriend Celia James, also deceased of New Orleans. His grandmother is Bella Black. Blade is now part of The Blackmon family and Blackmon Ranch. In honor of my deceased brother Blade Sr. I will personally donate significantly to The Sickle Cell Foundation and match other donations. Any questions can be directed to Sylvester Beeman, Public Relations Manager for Blackmon Ranch, if it's legal, Anastasia Bla —Anastasia Wright. Bleek walked away followed by Anastasia and Blade. *He almost said Anastasia Blackmon.* Anastasia thought. *My man claims me.*

¥¥¥¥¥

Marie threw her bourbon glass at her television.

¥¥¥¥¥

Bella Black smiled. *My grandson will have what I signed away for my son.*

CHAPTER THIRTEEN

Bleek's eyes opened at nine am. He stared at the clock, wondering why it didn't go off at six and all the activities of the day before filled his memory. After the press conference Frederick assured him he would handle everything the next day and Anastasia reinforced it. She told them she would be working from Bleek's. He got up and went to the bathroom. A tired smile covered his face when he saw a washcloth, towel and his toiletries spread out on the sink. It felt good to have a woman, a beautiful, accomplished woman who cared that much about him. He quickly used the toilet, showered and got dressed.

The scent of food assaulted his nostrils as he headed to the kitchen. Blade was at the table with a plate filled with pancakes, eggs and three fried pork chops. Anastasia walked towards him, with a mug of coffee, kissing him first.

"Good morning." She said before going to get his plate.

"Hey baby. Good morning Blade."

"Good morning sir."

"Blade, we are going to have to work on the sir thing. I know calling me Uncle Bleek might be too soon…" Bleek said as he sat at the table across from his nephew.

Anastasia listened as she filled Bleek's plate. There were so many things to learn and to navigate. Blade was calling her Ms. Anastasia and that was fine with her.

"I can call you Uncle Bleek, I just didn't want to assume nothing." Blade said. He turned to Anastasia who was placing Bleek's plate in front of him. "Are you Auntie, Ms. Anastasia?"

"Only if you're not on some Wakanda thing and trying to be funny young man." She answered. Blade blushed furiously. Bleek's eyes were on him. *He's already crushing on my woman.*

"And only if you're not flirting with my woman." Bleek said. "We are trying to grow a family here, I don't want to have to lay hands on you." His voice held just enough humor.

"Uncle Bleek, she's as old as my mama." Blade said but thought, *she don't look like my mama.*

"Boy, I'm the one who will slap you around if you call me old." Anastasia said. She sat next to Bleek with her coffee.

"She will too, she can box and carries a Sig." Bleek said. Blade's face was bright red.

"Y'all different." Blade said. "Y'all live like this but act like regular people. I expected to get thrown out but I had to come."

"Anastasia kind of uppity sometimes but I'm what they call the blackest cowboy because why should I have any airs about me. I'm not trying to impress anyone. I'm just me."

"Blade, you are going to see your uncle get drop-kicked and the sad thing is all those cowboys of his will be on my side. He's got about twelve more times to call me out my name. Watch and see."

Blade shook his head but Bleek winked at her before biting into his pork chop.

"She's uppity and bougie but can fry some pork chops." Bleek said.

"That's ten—I'm going to work in the other room."

She snatched the half chop out of his hand and left the room. They both followed her with their eyes.

"Blade, I need you to think of what you want to do with your future. You can go to college of course. While in college, I'll need you to work here with Frederick. He's the horse man. I'll pay you a grand a week for forty hours work and you will work." Bleek said. Blade's eyes widened at the money.

"Uncle Bleek, I want to know everything you and—and my dad's father knew about horses. I would like to take classes too. I'm real good with computers."

"Cool, we will work on that next week but we have rodeo in three days and that's our focus this week. Can you ride?"

"No sir."

"That's first, Frederick will give you a horse and train you. For the next three days you will go in with me at seven and spend your days with Frederick." Bleek looked him over in his baggy jeans and New Orleans Saints jersey. "Frederick will also give you more fitting clothing. Those baggy jeans too loose and your throwback too valuable. We get dirty on the ranch. Robert will get you a charge card and banking account as well. The rest we will figure out as we go."

"Yes sir." Excitement filled Blade's belly. He hadn't known what to expect but this sure as hell wasn't it. When Bella told him they were rich, he had no idea what rich meant. This was a different black world.

"One more thing, there is one way to lose me and that's to play me. I'll change your life but you better always be on the up and up with me blood or not."

Blade heard and felt Bleek's words and saw the truth in his eyes.

"Uncle Bleek, I'm no fool." Blade said, his head lifted his gaze direct. "I know y'all looked me up, I ain't never been in trouble. I was too busy taking care of my dad. My grandma didn't play, I got whooping."

"Good. I'm a straight up man and I respect straight up men. I like everything out there.

And I didn't look you up but I know my woman did. She's about me and so are those who work for me. I'm about her and those who work here. We are leaving in an hour." Bleek said. He finished his food and went to Anastasia.

"I'm going to take Blade to the ranch and get him on a horse. Are you going in?" Blake asked Anastasia.

"I was but your mom wants to talk to me, I'm going there."

"Are you up to that?"

"I am. If I'm going to be part of this family, everything comes with it. Bleek, I met you less than five months ago but this, us, is real. Your mom is part of you. Do you think she will ever acknowledge Blade?"

Bleek's heart swelled looking down at the woman he loved who loved him like that.

"We are real. You're the most real thing in my life Anastasia. And my heart is already feeling Blade. Did you think he was my kid before you knew?"

"You know it. That boy looks like you spit him out."

"How would that have been?"

"I don't even know. If you had a son nineteen years before me, no harm no foul but if you were hiding a kid, then Bleek Blackmon, we would have had a problem. However, we don't so all is well." Bleek grabbed her out of her chair and kissed her hard and thoroughly.

"Okay Auntie, I see you." Bleek said and ran from the room.

¥¥¥¥¥

Marie was in her dressing grown when Anastasia arrived. Her face was scrubbed clean and a scarf expertly tied around her hair. She looked years younger but Anastasia knew she would never go out natural. Her hair, makeup and clothing had to be done and appropriate. Without asking she poured a mug of tea for Anastasia and placed store bought pound cake on a plate. They sat in an over furnished room called the parlor. Marie talked and Anastasia listened.

"I met Bleek Jr. when I was thirty and he was thirty-three. He was as handsome as the devil and even more charming. I was engaged to Raymond but after meeting Bleek Jr. that was done. He dated me more than four years before asking me to marry him. I was a career woman, managing an exclusive clothing boutique for a Jewish couple. My mom worked for the same family as a housekeeper. I had never met anyone like the Blackmons. Bleek Sr. was half Native American and half Negro, his mother Black. He owned a few acres compared to what it is now but land has always been wealth. He approved of me for his son but his wife wanted a high yellow woman, like her, for her only child. She said it to my face. That's how it was back then. But I didn't care, I was in love." Marie paused to sip her tea and stare off into the past.

"I know he dicked around, I didn't know a man who didn't but when he told me about that boy, that was my line in the sand. He asked if he could bring him here." That shocked Anastasia but made sense. "I told him it was that boy or me and Bleek. Bleek was my ace in the hole because Bleek Jr. loved his son more than anything, including this land. He bought them a home and started sending monthly checks. I personally got her to sign something to keep her mouth shut. When the boy was about three she said he was sick. By then Bleek Jr. had cut all ties. He also had a vasectomy, partly to screw around and not get caught and to punish me for not allowing him to bring that boy here. I don't care how y'all feel but I would do the same thing again. But chickens always come home to roost and I figure you know once my son has made up his mind, that's it. The good thing for you is he's honorable. You're good for him Anastasia. I embrace you fully but I'm not ready to with my husband's grandson. Judge me if you must."

"No judgement here. I understand how you feel. I also understand why Bleek is embracing him, Blade is his blood. Bleek, Blade Jr. and Blade are innocents in all of this."

Marie's mouth turned down a bit but she nodded.

"I had to say that to you. I'm taking a leave from the ranch, I'll let you know when or if I resume my duties. I'm three years from eighty, it might be time to retire and live it up." Anastasia held up her mug.

"I'll drink to that." Anastasia said. She sat quietly with Marie until the older woman told her she needed a nap. Anastasia kissed the side of her face before leaving. She needed to go see Sage and Joel.

¥¥¥¥¥

"Where is your ring?" Sage asked after letting Anastasia in and hugging her. "Your man called and asked Joel for your hand in marriage."

"Hello mom, where is my daddy?" Anastasia asked. Joel walked in the room, hugging her.

"Hey baby, I hear crazy things going on at the ranch."

"Just a little." She followed her parents to the kitchen and told them as much as she could without breaking any confidences.

"I bet Ms. Marie is beside herself but I'm on her side with this. If any children show up looking like you, Joel is going to meet his maker." Sage said, eyeing him as if he did something.

Joel sat back in his chair, throwing up his hands.

"This isn't about me Sage. Besides I'm a mere retired principal not a billionaire or whatever Bleek is. This my love is above my head and pay grade."

"You heard what I said." Sage said. "How are you Anastasia?"

"I'm great. Friday is rodeo, Bleek wants you there as his special guests. On Sunday we are driving out to meet Bella Black, Blade's grandmother."

"Anastasia, please tell me you and Bleek aren't bringing that woman back to flaunt in Marie's face." Sage said. *She became team Marie with the quickness.* Anastasia thought.

"Mom, Bleek loves his mom, he wouldn't do that. He simply wants to meet her, thank her and offer her assistance. Please get out *your* feelings, this isn't about you."

"Anastasia, don't make me slap you out of your feelings." Sage said.

"Mom, seriously? You have made this personal, slap me, for what? Dad?"

"I'll say this, women bond over shit that has nothing to do with them. Sage Wright is doing that." Sage sucked her teeth but changed the subject.

"So, when are the nuptials?" Sage asked.

"We haven't gotten there yet. He proposed last night in he midst of chaos."

"He's serious baby girl, he called me. He's a good man, proven even more by how he's treating this kid Bleek owes nothing." Joel said.

"Dad, he is. Blade is a good kid. He spent the last three years taking care of his dad and doing well in school. I'm grateful Roger hired me to replace him I couldn't have dreamed up *that* man or my life."

"That's exactly what he said about you." Joel said. "That's all a parent hopes their daughter gets in a husband, right Sage."

"Right Joel, but don't sign a prenuptial." Sage had to say. Anastasia groaned, making Joel chuckle.

"Mom, do you have any idea how you sound?"

"I sure do, like a mom and future grandmother looking out for hers."

"Dad, your wife is outlandish." Joel winked at Anastasia. Sage rolled her eyes at both of them.

¥¥¥¥¥

For the first time in years Anastasia went home and decided to take a nap. After the past two days with the Blade issue and listening to Marie and Sage she felt exhausted. She awoke four hours later to Bleek sitting next to the bed holding her hand. They exchanged keys shortly after they started seeing each other.

"Hey." She murmured.

"Hey. Are you okay? I phoned you, mom and your dad after going to the house. This was my final check before putting out an all points bulletin."

"I'm good. This was closer after leaving my folks. My phone is in my purse. Sorry."

"No, I'm sorry. You've been exposed to a lot due to being with me. We were in the midst of the Gloss debacle and then this. How was mom and your folks?"

"Dad is dad and Marie and Sage are Marie and Sage. How was Blade's first day?"

"Every muscle in his body aches. He's a natural rider and hard worker. He's taken to Frederick and him to Blade. At forty-five Frederick has three girls, all very girly. Blade is officially his dude."

Great." She started to get up but Bleek lifted the hand he was holding. On her finger was the largest diamond she ever saw. She yelled and held her hand up, grinning at her rock.

"Is that okay, fiancé?"

"Okay? Bleek, it's perfect. Almost as beautiful as us." He watched her looking at the ring and him.

"Nothing is as beautiful as us. Do you feel up to coming home with me? I dropped Blade off there."

"Not before you kiss me like I'm your fiancé." She murmured, biting into her soft lower lip.

Bleek stood and started slowly undressing. Her eyes focused on his hard beauty. He snatched off the covers and saw her in only her panties. He got in bed with her and pulled off her panties with his teeth and pushing her legs open, leading with his tongue. He licked and nibbled her to ecstasy before lifting her legs and plunging inside.

CHAPTER FOURTEEN

The rodeo was one of the best attended the ranch had. Sylvester was proving to be worth his salary and more. Blade didn't participate in anything but was front and center with Frederick and the horse riders. After four days he looked ranch born in his wrangler jeans, blue button down shirt, his Bleek Brand cowboy boots and hat. The best part is he looked happy. Marie was noticeably absent from the festivities but wished Bleek a successful event via a phone call. Bleek was pleased. The headlines the following morning read.

BLEEK BLACKMON III does things his way.

The 21st Century ranch owner and cowboy known as the Blackest cowboy and not just because of that velvety complexion but because he owns it all and stays in the black with the money—honey, not to mention being in love with a Black woman. A woman who rumor has it scored a two million per year contract sight unseen by the COWBOY. And she now sports a rock the size of a marble on her engagement finger. In addition he has taken in his nephew who looks good in the saddle as well. It just is not right to be that wealthy and good looking with all that rich melanin. But missing from yesterday's festivities was the grande dame of Blackmon Ranch, Marie Smythe Blackmon. No one is saying why but we figure it ain't easy accepting your dearly departed's secret offspring into the fold but who knows, rich people are different.

It is more and more diverse these days as well, we saw a couple of women wranglers and the new Public Relations Lead is a big gay man who claims he has never been in anyone's closet. Honeys, cowboying is not what it once was but we are here for all of it.

¥¥¥¥¥

Anastasia read the article on their drive to New Orleans. She didn't mention it. The drive was twelve hours one way and she loved road trips. Bleek gave all but a skeleton staff the week off after the rodeo to rest and recover. It was spring time and everything amped up including the harvesting of two thousand acres of fruit and vegetables which fed the ranch and the surrounding community at no charge to them. Nathaniel and his crew were also at their busiest because they auctioned cattle. A percentage were also donated to the community.

They left at five am, stopping several times for food and restroom breaks. Anastasia offered to drive but Bleek wouldn't hear of it. Blade was so exhausted and sore he slept most of the time though he offered to drive.

"Y'all tried to kill the youngun?" Anastasia asked, peering at Blade in the rear view mirror.

"Not at all. When all those muscles get really ripped, he will be flexing. I was about twelve when I got to work with the horses. Dad's horse guy at that time was a hard ass named Butch Jones. I couldn't walk after my first week but couldn't wait to ride again. Being a cowboy is not for everyone. Blade's going to be a badass."

"Ayyye." Blade murmured tiredly.

They stopped in Baton Rouge, two hours away. Anastasia asked if they could get a room and stay overnight. She was tired and— she wanted boiled crabs from Capital City, a place she visited with her parents more than twenty years earlier on a trip. Bleek was open to it.

Bleek and Blade had platters of fried seafood, Anastasia devoured a dozen jumbo crabs and ordered three dozen shipped in a week.

"My daddy would have loved you Auntie." Blade said. "He could eat boiled crabs everyday." Bleek inhaled that information about the brother he never met. Blade shared his dad loved young blues singers, black leather converses and thick women with deep southern accents. The only way he would know his brother was through Blade's memory.

"I love them. Louisiana has the best in my crab eating opinion. Followed by Florida. I need them boiled not steamed." Anastasia said.

Later that night in bed Bleek asked Anastasia if Marie mentioned Blade Sr. during their conversation. Anastasia hesitated, she didn't want to widen the rift between Bleek and his mother or break a confidence. "Robert told me it was her; according to him dad was going to raise him but mom threatened to leave him."

"Bleek, talk to your mom about this and what happened. I think Bella will share her perspective also."

Bleek pulled her closer.

"A loyal woman. Another reason to love you."

"Confidences shared out of context causes more dissension. That's not my thing. Mom and I have all kinds of differences and the *two* of us hash it out. But, you are now my sounding board if anyone is too aggravating and I'm here for that with you."

"Thank you." He whispered near her ear. He sounded as tired as she felt.

¥¥¥¥¥

They arrived at Bella's at ten am. Bleek was pleased to see a large brick home on more than an acre of land. The home was clearly built in the 1980s but Bleek Sr. spared no expense in building it. It was easily 2500 hundred square feet and well maintained, it was surrounded on three sides by concrete fencing. *Thanks for this dad.* Bleek thought, looking around.

Bella walked out on the porch, watching them pull into her driveway. Blade wanted to surprise her. She was a stout, curvy woman with light brown skin, dreadlocks down her back and a ready smile. She appeared to be in her mid-fifties but they knew she was fifty-nine. She was wearing a long house dress. When Blade got out of the truck she raced down the steps into his arms. They heard her delighted laughter.

"Boy you look like a grown man with your haircut and in those clothes. Look at you." She said, her eyes drinking in her only grandchild from her only child. Blade blushed hard. He cut his huge Afro down considerably to short loose curls, faded on the sides. He ran his hand over his hair and took a cocky pose. Bella's giggles filled the air.

"Grandma, this is Uncle Bleek and his fiancé, Auntie Anastasia." Bella faced them and her face changed. Looking at Bleek was like seeing his father forty years ago. It was uncanny the resemblance. Bleek was forty to Bleek Jr's then forty three.

"Lord, you look like a ghost." Bella said. Bleek smiled, turning on the charm. The older woman blushed deep red. Blushing ran in the family.

"Ma'am, I'm Bleek III, meeting you is my pleasure. Anastasia and I wanted to let you know in person, Blade is in a safe place." Bella beamed before hugging Bleek. She embraced Anastasia saying, "you're a beautiful woman. Y'all looked better in person. I saw y'all on CNN and said them some good looking Negroes. Y'all just caught me. I returned from the fish creek an hour ago and got cleaned up. I got a tub full of bluegill and bass. Y'all eat fish?"

"Ms. Bella, not only do I eat fish, I'm a fisherman, I catch redfish and speckled trout. I'm also good at cleaning them." Bleek said. Bella's eyes raked over him in his expensive blue jeans and button down and didn't look convinced.

"If you say so but I have a man friend named Horace who scaled and gutted them at the creek. Y'all come in and I'm frying up a mess." She grabbed Blade's hand and they walked ahead. Bleek grinned at Anastasia who grinned back. She had been leery of surprising the woman but Blade knew his grandmother. She led them through a spacious living room into an even more spacious kitchen where her sink was filled with fresh fish. Bleek peeked in and held up two huge fish.

"These are mine." He said. Bella chuckled from deep in her belly.

"You got it. Blade get your uncle and auntie some sweet tea. I hope y'all didn't drive straight through."

"We didn't." Anastasia said. "We stopped in Baton Rouge."

"Grandma, she ate a grip of crabs even that yellow stuff, like daddy."

"Honey that boy of mine loved him some crabs. I can take 'em or leave em but I'll eat fresh, fried fish everyday except Sunday. On Sunday I want chicken, fried." She said, filling the air with her infectious laughter. "Blade, I baked a lemon pound cake early this morning before meeting Horace at the creek."

"Auntie loves cake too." Blade said.

"Sure do." Anastasia said. After giving them jars of tea, they watched Blade pull out a huge iron skillet and pour peanut oil in it.

"I'm so glad y'all accepted my boy. He needed to go somewhere different and have different experiences. Now me, I'm never leaving the bayou but I want him to live and do things. God is good, I know my Blade Sr. is resting in peace." Bella did a little praise dance that touched Bleek and Anastasia.

During the meal she told funny stories about her Blades. She shared that she was known as the cake and fish lady to add to her bottom line. She appeared to be a woman at peace with her life, accepting everything as God's choice. After dinner Anastasia walked outside and Blade drove to see friends leaving Bleek to talk to Bella.

"I know I can't fix what my dad did but I want to assist you in any way I can."

"Bleek, I was with your daddy knowing he had a wife and child. I was twenty and he was —I didn't deny him. When I got pregnant he bought me this home and provided for us. I know he wanted to take my child but I would never have allowed that and not because of no money either. I expected the money to stop once Blade turned eighteen but it went on until your daddy died. The last time I saw him Blade was four. He stopped coming and I didn't chase him, he wasn't mine to chase. He was good to us. Your mama showed up one time and got me to sign a paper. I signed it and stood by it but after my boy died just over a month ago, I told my grandson. He deserved to know. Blade lived twenty years longer than the doctors said and gave us that boy. I ain't got no complaints. This is my house and my land and I earn enough to stay fat." She said with more genuine laughter. Bleek admired her and gave her a check that made her eyes bug out.

"This is because you helped raise my nephew, who is a good man, no strings. Please accept it."

Tears filled Bella's eyes. She picked up the check and reached for Bleek's hand.

"Thank you Bleek. Your daddy was a good man, just one with weaknesses like many men. Remember him well and your brother lacked for nothing except time and that's determined by God."

"I receive that."

They spent two nights with Bella, Bleek and Anastasia slept in Blade Sr.'s room. The next morning Bella, Bleek and Blade went fishing before the sun was up while Anastasia slept.

That evening Horace, a few years younger than Bella but clearly enamored with her brought over boiled crabs and all the fixings. Anastasia surprised them all with her card playing and trash talking skills beating Horace in a game called Tunk. Bleek, a bid whist and spades player had never heard of the game but was constantly surprised at the layers to his fiancé.

Bleek allowed Blade to drive the new truck back to Florida. Anastasia knew it meant it was now his. She was grateful to fly back after spending two more nights in a hotel in Baton Rouge with Bleek, no crabs that time just hot sex and relaxation.

"CHAPTER FIFTEEN

For the next three months at Blackmon Ranch it was harvest and cattle sales time. Everyday there were auctions, sales and celebrations. More was accomplished during that time then any time of the year and everyone worked ten to twelve hours daily.

"He came on at the right time." Bleek said to Anastasia watching Blade assisting Nathaniel get cattle onto a truck. It was the last of the cattle sales for the season. It was early morning and in a few hours there would be a manager meeting.

"He did. He hardly looks like the same lost kid who showed up four months ago. His confidence is off the charts and he looks ranch born and bred."

"It's that DNA baby. He's a Blackmon, with all that entails. He's moving into the house behind mine on the property." About a half mile behind Bleek's was a two bedroom house he lived in until he built his current home. "I've seen him with a couple of women and he isn't bringing that in my house."

"I'm sure because young Blade is a catch and easy on the eyes."

"Watch your mouth Anastasia. I'm a man with feelings."

Anastasia draped her arm through his.

"I know but the boy looks just like you with fresh new muscles." She teased. Bleek popped her on her butt, hard.

"Don't test me woman."

"If you gonna hit it like that, I might." She said and strutted away towards her office. She glanced over her shoulder.

"You know I'm watching you." He yelled.

They decided on getting married the week after Christmas which was in six months. He didn't want to wait but acquiesced because Sage insisted with Anastasia's approval on a big wedding. That would give them a year of getting to know each other.

All I know is I love her, want to marry her and get at least two babies. Bleek thought.

¥¥¥¥¥¥

Marie was in the conference room when Bleek arrived. It was the first meeting she attended since Blade came on. Blade didn't attend meetings, he wasn't a manager. The only add-on was Sylvester who had been a boon for the ranch. He wasn't contracted like Gloss but an employee of the brand. Bleek kissed Marie's forehead before taking his seat. Everyone was there except Anastasia and Robert who walked in five minutes later.

"Sorry, we're late." Anastasia said. "We wanted the most recent figures." She said as Robert passed out the quarterly reports.

Bleek glanced at them but Anastasia informed him earlier they had the best quarter in history.

"Good morning." Bleek said after everyone was seated. "The past three months have been phenomenal in every way, though at times it looked sideways but those of you have been around knows that's ranch life. I'm grateful to everyone for hard work and dedication and your bonuses which Robert assured me will hit your accounts by day's end will reflect that. Nathaniel kudos to you and your team for an outstanding quarter."

"Thank you and I have to shout out Frederick's protege, Blade, that young brother works hard. He's a cowboy for real. Frederick, I want to keep him."

"Sorry, my brother but he's a horseman." Frederick said. Anastasia watched them, her eyes lighting on Marie who looked bored.

"Also, kudos to Sylvester for being the PR guru this place needed. You make us look good." Sylvester bowed. "Robert, do you have anything?"

"The reports speak for themselves. Everything is stellar."

"Anastasia, there are no words to express what you added to me and this ranch over the past nine months. I have always felt timing is divine because you arrived on this ranch and in my life right on time. That's why you're—my woman, I love you and everything you bring." The fellows started stomping and whooping. Anastasia stood and did her own bow.
"Thanks my love. That sounds so unprofessional but you are my love Bleek Blackmon, but we have a problem." The room quieted and Bleek's heart stilled a bit.

"A problem?"

"Yes, with our wedding date. I'm going to have our baby. I'm about six weeks…" before she could complete her speech, Bleek was out of his chair, holding her in his arms.

"We are having a baby?" He asked.

"We are having a baby in about seven and a half months." She said, staring into his eyes.

"We are having a baby! A baby! A baby!" Bleek said. He placed Anastasia on the floor and did a step move filled with joy. His brothers in the room joined him, stepping around Anastasia who was giggling.

"Hello." Marie said.

Everyone turned to face her, having forgotten she was in the room. "That's the best news this old broad has heard in a long time. Congratulations. Anastasia you need to tell your folks." There was a knock on the door and Sage and Joel walked in. Joel had cigars.

"Bleek I had to tell them." Anastasia said. "That's why I was late."

"Hell yea. This is a celebration." Bleek said, grabbing one of the cigars and placing it between his teeth. He pulled Anastasia close and danced her around the room. Blade walked in ten minutes later. Frederick texted him.

"Congratulations Uncle Bleek and Auntie!" He said. He hugged them both.

"Thanks Nephew." Bleek and Anastasia said at the same time. Marie looked away, she couldn't look at Blade. Sage took her hand and squeezed it.

¥¥¥¥¥

After the announcement and congratulations only Bleek, Anastasia and Marie were left in the room. Sage and Joel were with everyone else joining in the ranch festivities.

"Bleek, I'm happy for you son. However, I'm moving off the property. I'm almost eighty and my husband and his father died at eighty on this ranch." Bleek listened a huge lump in his throat. "But I'm likely going to live to be a hundred but it won't be here. Raymond has asked me to marry him and I've accepted. Bleek—I need this. Of course, it will be after your nuptials. Well, it was going to be before but since we're having a baby…" she said and chuckled. Bleek felt relief fill him.

"Mom, live your life. Your home will always be there. I know you didn't ask for it but you have my blessing."

"Son, that means everything. It's your turn now son, you and your family. Anastasia, you're a prize, never forget that. Bleek, don't you allow this ranch to make you forget either. She's your biggest blessing."

"I know mom."

"Thanks Mom Marie." Anastasia said.

"Raymond is out there somewhere, wherever the brisket it. I'm going to join him." They stood embracing her.

"It's been eight months, not quite nine for the record books." Anastasia said.

"It has but I wouldn't change any of it, not even the crazy parts."

"Me either. Sorry, I told mom first."

"I ain't tripping. That's my baby in there." Bleek said, placing his hand on her belly. "What are we going to do about a wedding?"

"We will have a ceremony here in a few weeks. After our baby is born, we will have the biggest, most lavish shindig anyone has ever seen."

"That's what's up." Bleek said, placing his forehead on hers. "You changed my life, my world."

"I'm yours man, that's how I do. Let's go party with our people." She stood and reached for his hand.

They walked outside to a huge crowd, yelling congratulations, led by Blade.

Boo'd Up by Ella Mai, a hit from a few years earlier filled the air. Nathaniel was on the music.

"They are boo'd up and it looks good on em." Nathaniel said on the mike. "Y'all know boss man pulled rank on me and stole her."

"You never had a chance handsome." Anastasia said as Bleek danced her around the dance grounds.

"At least she called me handsome." Nathaniel said, cranking up the music. All Bleek heard was Anastasia's heart thumping against his.

The music changed and a crowd joined them, including Sage and Joel who loved dancing. Blade danced with two women. Marie looked on from the periphery.

That's the future of this place. She thought. *As it should be.* Raymond wrapped his arm around her and kissed the side of her face.

"This is beautiful Marie and Bleek Jr. would be proud."

"Raymond, I know. He raised Bleek for this. My part in it has ended, without regrets. Take me home with you."

Raymond proudly led her to his car. He waited more than forty years for her.

¥¥¥¥¥

All partied out, Bleek and Anastasia rested on his balcony. She was lying between his legs, his hand on her stomach, cradling their baby.

"Anastasia, I didn't want to be married or have a kid, even knowing once I died all of this would end with me. I can't even say why now. Perhaps, it's being a cowboy who mostly just wanted to get on his horse and ride. Or it was watching my dad treat my mom secondary to the land and to me. I convinced myself she was happy being his wife and my mom but I know better now." Anastasia's eyes were closed as he spoke, she knew he needed to talk and she to listen. "But you were only here a few days when I wanted to murder Nathaniel, my friend because he was interested in you. I drug you into a photo shoot, I didn't want to do because I wanted you, needed to be close to you. From the day you walked in my office—it was you. Now, here we are, I'll be forty-one in a couple of months and you're pregnant with my seed—my son, I already know. I want to be the best husband, father and man I can be for you, for him or them. Nothing else is as important as this, not this ranch, this land, nothing."

"I know Bleek. I always wanted a kid, maybe two but as I grew more successful and got older I thought probably not. Day one I thought you were the most beautiful man I ever saw but an asshole surrounded by men, horses and your mama. I thought, hell no but the day on the horses, I saw and felt you, the man you were. You are a cowboy and I fell hard for you—I mean hard. I want this and you. Do you know what we, you and I can do with our resources? We can change things Bleek."

"We can, so, I'm the blackest cowboy, what's your title?"

"I've been Bleek's woman since you claimed me, I guess that makes me the blackest cowboy's wife."

"That sounds good, though I was thinking, Anastasia Blackmon, Ranch Co-owner but whatever it is, it's us." *Co-owner?* Anastasia thought. *We will discuss that later.*

"Anastasia, I know you heard me. We will own and run this ranch together. That's what being my wife will mean. Wrap your mind and heart around it."

"All in due time but right now I want you to come out of those boxers and I'm going to ride my favorite stallion. For the next week, it's recreation cause the procreation is already done." She stood up and over him, pulling the shirt she was wearing over her head and tossing it. He slid down his boxers, his hardness springing free, she slowly slid down on him, inch by inch, pulling him inside, their eyes locked.

"Ride then…"

CHAPTER SIXTEEN

Bleek was standing at the west corral when he saw Anastasia fast gallop up on Mocha. He felt as if his head were going to explode. Before she could get off the horse, he unleashed.

"Anastasia, what the hell do you think you're doing? You're risking my baby, riding." Veins stood out on his forehead.

She got off the horse, pushed him out of the way and walked across the yard towards her office. He raced after her and grabbed her arm. She did a move with her leg that landed him on the ground, hard. She stepped over him and continued her stride. Frederick raced over but Bleek was already on his feet.

"Man, you okay?"

"Hell no, did you know she was riding?" Bleek asked, his voice sounding dangerous.

"Yes, according to her and her doctor, she can ride. She sure can flip a brother." Bleek glared at him but took off behind Anastasia who was halfway to the office. He heard Frederick's chuckling behind him.

"Did auntie just drop Unk?" Blade asked walking up behind Frederick.

"Dropped and strode off."

"That's his shoota right there."

"Big facts. Let's get to work before he takes it out on our ass."

"Word."

Bleek got to Anastasia's office just as she slammed the door. He waited a few minutes before walking inside. She was sitting behind her desk, her expression furious.

"Don't come in here with your shit Bleek Blackmon. You might talk crazy to your cowboys but not to me. Yelling like you lost your mind." Her voice wavered and he realized she was on the edge of tears. *Oh hell.*

"Baby, I panicked. I saw you on the horse and could only think of you falling and hurting you and the baby."

"Bleek, I'm seven weeks pregnant which means for the six weeks prior I was pregnant and riding. I'm pregnant not an invalid and I wouldn't risk *our baby* or myself. If you had looked you would have seen I have a new saddle with leather fitted over my thighs and higher on my back for added protection."

Bleek rubbed his hand over his face. He hadn't noticed any of that, just her flying on Mocha.

"I might have overreacted but you have to see my side."

"You *might* have and I *have* to?"

"Damn it woman, I overreacted and I probably will again. I'm a cowboy who spent most of his life in the presence of hard heads and roughnecks. You know you dropped me on my ass in front of my man and nephew."

"You yelled at me in front of them, that was your playground, I played. I will again if you come at me wrong. Did I kill you?" She snapped. He walked up to the desk and leaned over it, in her face.

"You better be glad I'm busy today or I would take you home right now and give you what you really crave." He said and stepped back. He glanced at her nipples hardening under her Blackmon Ranch t-shirt. "Yea, that's what I thought." He said cockily before kissing her and leaving her office. She threw up her middle finger to his back.

Bleek walked back to the stalls. Frederick and Blade were staring at him.

"I'm not paying y'all to stand around looking at me. We got horses to train." He growled. They snapped into action.

¥¥¥¥¥

At the end of an exhausting work day Bleek's phone buzzed as he prepared to go home. A smile covered his face when he saw a message from Anastasia.

Please come to the house, the house off the ranch. I'm preparing your favorite foods, I'll have your favorite beverage after your favorite fiancé joins you in a tub full of oils and bubbles. Do not take this as an apology because I did nothing wrong but as me loving my man enough to be the better person… your woman, Anastasia.

Bleek's laughter filled the air as he hurried to his truck. He was trying to figure out how to fix things but she was always ahead of him.

¥¥¥¥

Bleek allowed Anastasia to cater to him. He felt he should be doing the catering but she insisted. After his bath, she served him his favorite medium porterhouse steak, baked potato and greens with *The MacCallan* 18 year old scotch with two ice balls.

"I could get used to this." Bleek said. After their meal Anastasia was curled up in his lap. "I love how you apologize."

"I am *not* apologizing. I just felt sorry you got dropped in front of your man and your nephew."

"That was wrong. They talked trash all day. And of course it just had to be Frederick and Blade who saw it. The others would have at least pretended to have some respect."

"You grabbed me—that's how that ends up."

"You're right on that. I shouldn't have grabbed you but I panicked. I don't want anything to happen to you or our baby. I apologize for that part."

"As you should, especially when I'm already hot. I know it wasn't in anger though or you would be laid up in the hospital. I need you to trust me. I'm always going to do the right thing by us—all of us."

"I know, yet I'm bound to get it wrong again. As long as we're here, together, I can deal with anything."

"Then, we are dealing, fiancé."

¥¥¥¥¥

Sage and Marie were on a Zoom call discussing the wedding. Marie was in Ocala with Raymond and Sage in Gainesville.

"Sage, I have to ask how old are you? I know Anastasia is going to be thirty-eight soon." Marie said. Over the past week they started conversing mostly about the wedding that would now be at the ranch in a few weeks and the baby.

"I'm almost seventy-one." Sage responded. She was used to being thought of as younger. She worked at staying fit and attractive for herself and Joel. She saw the surprise on Marie's face. Because Anastasia was thirty-eight, many guessed fifty-eight or nine. "I love working out and Joel gives great sex."

"I remember great sex." Marie said with a sigh. "Bleek Jr. was a slim man not muscular but honey he was hung like one of them horses and talented with it. He was eighty when he passed and we had sex the night before. We never stopped the loving, just slowed down a little." Sage listened quietly. She loved details. "Raymond was good until I had great. Now he's rare with sex but he has other talents; besides I'm damn near eighty so I'll take that." Marie said so dry, Sage wept with laughter.

"I hear you. I didn't think we would get along," Sage said.

"Me either because not eating beef is just offensive but you were so kind after Bleek's nephew arrived. I appreciated that. Anastasia told me she was sorry I was going through this but Bleek had her loyalty. I knew when I met her she would be a good match for Bleek —but that day I knew she loved him as him and though I wanted her on my side, I loved that for him that she was on his. I knew he loved her. She's a firecracker."

"You have no idea. She's a daddy's girl, so we were always squared off. Raising outspoken, independent children often backfires."

"Who are you telling? Bleek never listened to anything he didn't agree with. But Anastasia, she's his handler."

"She is. Are you ever going to talk to Blade, he's a great kid?" Sage asked. Marie hesitated but decided to answer. It was nice talking to another woman. Living on a ranch didn't bring many women into your life and most of Marie's family were deceased.

"Probably not, not intentionally anyway. I'm not required to and no one can persuade me to. He's not my family. That's the thing everyone is behaving as if I'm rejecting my blood—not my husband's bastard's child. They should all be grateful I'm not taking Bella to court. I have a contract she signed to never disclose her son's parentage to anyone." A look of horror crossed Sage's features. Marie chuckled at her expression. "I thought about it but Bleek would disown me and now there's going to be a baby. The truth is I didn't care what my husband did out of the state, I just wasn't going to have it in my face. People can think what they want and even quote scriptures but I'm not doing it."

"Marie, don't even think like that. Because Bleek and his attorney, Anastasia would come for you and you don't want that."

Marie threw her head back, trilling with delighted laughter.

"Indeed I don't. I have to go wake Raymond up so he can go to bed. It's nice chatting with you."

"Same here. Rest well."

She's salty as hell but I get it. Why if you don't have to? Sage thought. *Joel had better never —his payoff would have been to me after I cracked his skull and left him.*

Sage got up and walked into the family room to see what Joel was doing. He was bopping his head with headphones on. He saw her and pulled the headphones off.

"Whatever it is Sage, leave me out of it." He said, pulling the headphones back on. He knew she was on a call with Marie. She threw up her middle finger at him. He blew her a kiss.

CHAPTER SEVENTEEN

Bleek called a meeting after the manager meeting with a list of who would be there, him, Anastasia, Marie and Robert. Anastasia was surprised but Marie wasn't. She knew her son, how his mind worked and currently his heart.

Bleek, Marie and Robert were seated when Anastasia arrived. Bleek grinned at the snug dress she was wearing, at nine weeks she was about showing off what she called her pooch. It was barely noticeable but she wanted the world to see and that was exactly what Bleek wanted. The world to know. The day before, Sylvester announced the small wedding at the ranch in a week and that they were expecting a baby at the end of the year. Juan walked in behind her with tea and a bowl of chopped fruit, things she was currently craving. There was always food in meetings but Juan went above and beyond for Anastasia.

"I'm calling this meeting because I'm getting married in a week and becoming a father in less than seven months. I'm restructuring how the ranch is owned. First I'll say why and then how." He looked around at the three in attendance and only Anastasia was focused fully on him. "This ranch is thousands of acres that started as a couple hundred. My grandfather, the first Bleek inherited thirty and worked and bought hundreds more. When Bleek Sr. died this land became solely my father's. My grandmother owned the home she lived in and some acreage plus millions of dollars. The same occurred when my father died, he left it all to me except the house my mother lives in and the two hundred acres surrounding it, including more money than she will ever spend, mostly because she never picks up the tab." Marie snorted and Robert grinned. Anastasia popped fruit into her mouth. "But that changes with me. In eight days Anastasia will become, officially my wife and will be given thirty-five percent of Blackmon Ranch, we will be co-owners. The sixty-five percent will remain solely in the hands of those of Blackmon blood. No one will ever take anything from my wife, the woman I chose and who chose me because of her blood or lack thereof." He paused and did another perusal. Robert was smiling, Marie looked bored and Anastasia's eyes were filled though she was still eating her fruit. He watched her chew thoughtfully then wipe her hands and mouth.

"Mom Marie, how do you feel about this?" Anastasia asked.

"Bleek is doing what he should do. I understood when marrying Bleek Jr. this would never be mine but I would be cared for and I am. My parents were housekeepers and I now own two hundred acres of prime real estate and way more money than I will ever use, even if I picked up tabs. I also know my son is protecting you because honestly if Bleek died before me, I might not do by you what he's doing and if you live a long life together then young Blade might not. This kind of money and land changes people.

When Bleek is eighty and you're seventy-seven, Blade will be fifty-nine with a wife and who knows how many sons…his loyalty will not be to you. Not that he won't love you but that's how it works. Anastasia, my dear, you have done what no other Blackmon wife could, got one of them to love *you* more than the name or the land. I can only applaud that." Marie said. Hot tears splashed down Anastasia's face as she turned to face Bleek. He was watching her with wet eyes.

"That's it." Bleek said. "Anastasia, the beauty of it is I know you are marrying me for me which makes it easy for me to do this—for you." Bleek said, his voice husky.

"The beauty is Bleek is all of this is trappings. Beautiful trappings but what we are growing in here…" she touched her heart and "In here." She touched her belly. "Is everything to us. I can make money and buy land." They stared at each other communicating how they felt without touch. Marie and Robert walked out together.

"Are you okay?" Robert asked Marie once they were in the corridor.

"I'm better than okay. Now if I had been fifty, even sixty when this occurred I might have been a mess but now I know it's the right thing and Anastasia Wright is the right one. Bleek is a man and it brings me great joy he defines manhood differently than Sr. and Jr. If rolling over in one's grave is true then both those bastards are rolling and rolling."

Robert's chuckles filled the corridor. He didn't know Bleek Sr. but he knew for damn sure Bleek Jr. was rolling.

"Bleek is the man. In ten years, this place will be bigger but with those two at the helm and it will be doing better things. I've seen that the last fifteen years with just Bleek but a woman on your team and in your head and bed who is about you—they can own the world. That's why I've never been worried about the new generation. They have more knowledge and way more heart than we will ever have. Do you think Anastasia even knows how much he gave her in addition to the Bleek Blackmon brand that he owns aside from all of this?"

"She doesn't have a clue, that's the got-damn beauty of it. We need to send Roger a bonus for hiring her. Who the hell knew?"

"I'm guessing that's one of those God things." Robert said.

¥¥¥¥¥

It Ain't WRIGHT

Listen up lovelies, I have never been one to hate, so I'm not hating but it ain't WRIGHT do you hear me? Anastasia Wright soon to be Blackmon will make a hater out of a girl…A year ago Sis was the fly attorney with the hair, clothes and booty…see, we were like okay, Sis worked for that but uh, uh, Sis had to get the job, the man as in Bleek Black-MAN, the big ass ring, now she's going to marry him with a belly full of his baby...do y'all know how that baby got in there...Bleek put it there. Not fair...but that is not the main thing, rumor has if she will OWN part of the ranch as in, here is your wedding gift wifey, to do with as you wish because you ain't got enough...oh hell yeah, I'm a hater and you are too. If they change the name to the andAnastasiaRanch, I will diiiie. But I might be jealous but one thing I'm not is mad—we cannot be mad at a sister who's got it like that. We might wish to be but we just cannot. Because it ain't Wright.

Black News You Can Use

Laughter spilled from Anastasia's throat as she read the most recent blurb on her. She was getting a kick out of reading them. It was her life and this was part of it. Bleek was nodding beside her as she was surfing the internet.

"She said, "Do you know how that baby got there…Bleek put it there. This woman is a comedy writer."

"Who baby?" Bleek asked, his voice groggy.

"This Black News writer. She is hilarious."

"You read trash talking about you and applaud the writer…makes sense."

"Bleek, it's funny. She writes in a nonconformist, Sista girl way that's sharp and funny. I know some is mean but there's no denying her skills."

"If you say so."

"I do. When you go in the kitchen please bring me some tea and my fruit bowl."

Bleek squinted at her with one eye, her eyes were still perusing her laptop.

"Just for the sake of clarity, when you say when I go in the kitchen, that means you want me to go now because I wasn't going in the kitchen."

"It means when you go. If you're not going then I can just go." She said, not moving an inch.

"Oh, I'm going. Right now. I think I mastered that lesson."

She rolled her tongue out at him but didn't look his way. Bleek's dick stiffened.

"Two lessons…" Bleek said on his way to get what she wanted. He was learning to pay close attention and ask questions directly where Anastasia was concerned. There were times of pure clarity when she said what she meant and meant what she said. Other times she implied with a look, You better figure some things out, partner. *I'm figuring it out.*

"Thanks Bleek." Anastasia said graciously as Bleek placed a tray on her lap. Her computer was closed and she was sitting with her feet tucked under her. "They're saying you're the new Black man, A conscious brother, about his Queen." *Another lesson loading.*

"One of the first things I told you Anastasia, day one, is I don't give a damn what they say or write about me. Whether it's good or bad because as my dad said, they didn't make me and they won't break me. That's why I don't read or believe any of the hype because today you're on and the next day you're off. That's how they make their money." Bleek said with feeling. There were a few minutes of silence.

"I'm glad you're that way because mostly I don't care and other times I care a lot— because it can't be because I worked hard, not just at my job but at staying grounded and grateful. For all of it. But in a few minutes I'm reduced to my looks, hair, ring, who they say I slept with and everything other than how hard it all is. But that's the game and I need you for those times when I'm bothered." Her full eyes met his and he saw part of her journey and not just the trappings. But the being placed apart from your peers by superficial things and being thought of no matter how successful you are as not having made it until you get the man and the bling. He pulled her into his arms.

"That's the man I'm trying to be and I'm taking the advanced course. I want to be your husband and lover first. I'm a simple man but I learn easy. Just tell me..."

"I will, most of the time. Except the times, I don't."

"That's fair. Now eat your fruit."

"I'm sick of it. My tastebuds acting up."

"Do you want me to get something else?"

"No, I just want to stay right here—like this."

I'm getting pretty good at this.

"If I change my mind, I'll tell you." She said, snuggling even closer.

School will always be in session but I love these benefits.

EPILOGUE

Bleek and Anastasia exchanged vows in front of their family, friends and staff. Everything in the barn was beautifully decorated and incorporated them both, there were the cowboy elements and urban professional mix. Bleek wore a black tailored suit with a cowboy hat he designed with the Bleek Brand emblem. Anastasia dress was short with a trail in sparkling white worn with stilettos and a white cowboy hat with a short veil. Their vows were unwritten and spoken from the heart with promises to love, respect and communicate honestly. The wedding was officiated by the Mayor of Center City, Pastor Jeremy Felipe. His wife attorney Aura Brown was also there, Bleek went to high school with Muhammad.

After the vows they partied for hours with their people before flying to Greece for an eighteen day honeymoon.

"In less than a year." Sage mused, her arm linked with Joel's as their daughter danced with her husband.

"Yes, because they were ready for each other. They were both successful on their own, had other lovers and associates and are likeminded in what matters. Your father told me that when I asked for your hand in marriage. I was thirty and you were twenty-nine and done just what they're doing on a smaller scale. You were in your seventh year of teaching and me my eighth and just promoted to assistant principal at thirty. We were ready and raised her to be ready."

"I guess if there's a formula, that's a good one."

"Look at us. Come on let's bust some moves!"

He led her to the floor when *Bustin' Loose* by Chuck Brown from the 1970s came on. They saw Marie allow Nathaniel to waltz her to the dance and busting loose with some moves they didn't expect.

Bleek and Anastasia were still slow dancing with their eyes closed in the midst of the dancers.

Raymond was on the periphery standing next to Roger, his long time friend.

"These young men are different." Raymond observed.

"A lot if them certainly are but Bleek is a different breed. Most young men would have never done what he's done and would've had all kinds of prenuptials in place. He's betting on her loving him as he loves her."

"That's good I guess but even the way they openly love their women, we didn't do that. They knew because of how we took care of them and in the alone times but look at him, he's as wide open as he can be." There was a tinge of admiration and bewilderment in Raymond's voice.

"Brother, I think that's the best part. I used to feel sad for Marie because Bleek Jr. was always making moves even at his wedding but she had no other expectations, that's how it was. I think a lot of those old ways and practices might have run it's course. I hope so and that young Blade is soaking it all up as will any kids of Bleek's especially any daughters. What he's done has insured his daughters future in the same way the elder Bleeks did his but neither would have left this ranch to a girl. I promise you if Marie hadn't had a son Blade's father would have grown up here no matter what Marie said. Bleek like I said is a different breed." Roger said and held up his glass. Raymond still looked skeptical but it wasn't his to understand.

At midnight, Bleek and Anastasia boarded a plane for Greece. After they were buckled in, Bleek asked, "are you ready Mrs. Blackmon?"

"I'm ready Mr. Blackmon." She responded as the plane taxied down the runway.

There will be other Blackmon Ranch books in the near future.

Angelia!

Made in the USA
Las Vegas, NV
04 June 2024

90750039R00138